GREASED LIGHTNING

"Just don't get no closer to that .45," Clancy said. "There is six of us, Adams." The foreman's face creased in a tight smile, around his cold, bullet-hard eyes.

"That is what I know, Clancy; and just like last time, I can hit you right in the belly, no matter how fast your men are. You figger that's a good swap?"

The foreman's small eyes dropped to the Gunsmith's right hand. It was just as Clint had planned it.

And with a speed that men had termed quicker than light, the Gunsmith's other hand—his left— flicked inside his shirt and was out and up with the Dean & Adams.

"Right now!" And that gun was pointing right at the foreman's heart.

Burt Clancy's eyes flicked to the right and left of the Gunsmith, then looked beyond him. "I got men all around you, Adams. Right and left and back." His voice was tight as a drumhead.

"I know that, Mr. Clancy. But I don't need anybody right and left and behind you. I've got you right here in front. . . ."

Also in THE GUNSMITH series

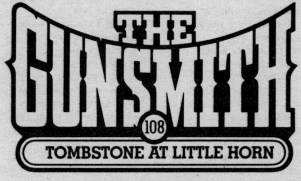

THE GUNSMITH

108

TOMBSTONE AT LITTLE HORN

J. R. ROBERTS

JOVE BOOKS, NEW YORK

THE GUNSMITH #108: TOMBSTONE AT LITTLE HORN

A Jove Book/published by arrangement with
the author

PRINTING HISTORY
Jove edition/December 1990

ISBN: 0-515-10474-4

Jove Books are published by The Berkley Publishing Group,
200 Madison Avenue, New York, New York 10016.
The name ''Jove'' and the ''J'' logo
are trademarks belonging to Jove Publications, Inc.

PRINTED IN THE UNITED STATES OF AMERICA

10 9 8 7 6 5 4 3 2 1

ONE

In the heated afternoon the land stretched dry as a bone under the vague yellow sun. It was an endless day; it seemed to have no beginning, no ending. To the human eye nothing moved, no change appeared. As though time were no longer there.

Yet, to the practiced observation of the man on the big black gelding, within the stillness there was movement, within the silence, sound. Not only the disappearing band of elk down by the breaks that seemed more shadow than substance, but the random ticking of the dry land, the whisper of the river twisting through cottonwoods and willows on its way to the little town at the far end of the long, wide valley that looked as though it had been thrown like an open gauntlet between the two mountain ranges. All this spoke the presence of a world.

Clint Adams could imagine the town, though he had never been there. He had been in Abilene, Ellsworth, Dodge, and dozens of the cattle centers and railroad end-of-track camps, those precursors of so many towns that grew like sage or prairie-dog villages out of some need that was only named long after they appeared: the definition in words of something that had been as random and as organic as seed tossed by the wind. Then, suddenly, something that had been there all along was seen, defined, and named, at which moment it became itself and its history, invented and reinvented, became the thought and feeling that met travelers and the endlessly appearing present. While finally the original, the organic, impulse of creation was forgotten, as those who came and went reacted more and more to the historical creation, the satisfying "history" of whatever town it happened to be. As indeed had happened, and was still happening, to the beautiful, wonderful country.

The Gunsmith, who too had been defined—and against his wish for himself—understood very well how the lie supplanted truth, creating legend—legend that bore the terrible capability of locking a man into its service. He knew all too well how the legend fashioned the manacles that not infrequently assured the death and failure of its prisoner.

But he was not dwelling on these reflections now. He was for sure the Gunsmith, though that was something applied to him by others. Inside, he was Clint Adams. He was himself. And he was content having himself, free in the awareness of the life coursing through him as he rode easily—and totally alert—toward the town known as Little Horn.

"Jumping Jesus!"
The sharp exclamation fell into the room like the

opening crack of a stampede. The speaker almost took a step forward, something in his body demanding compensation for the astonishment that had so suddenly threatened him.

"What? Who?" His companion stepped closer to catch what the first speaker had seen through the window. Like his friend, he was a stringy man, with big veins in his hands and a six-gun at his right hip.

"Jesus H. Christ!" This time the exclamation was softer, the speaker emphasizing more awe than surprise, as his bugging eyes followed the rider on the big black gelding easing in from the trail onto the town's main street.

His companion didn't repeat his question but simply followed the rider as the initial speaker was doing. He was chewing tobacco and now, not quite so overwhelmed as his friend, he began to scratch his crotch. "Somebody we know?" he asked finally.

"You can bet yer ass."

"Good news?"

"Depends why he's here."

"Could be you'd like to tell who this godalmighty feller is."

The rider was now out of sight. And the man who had recognized him turned back into the room, which was bare save for the two men, a round card table with a baize top, and half a dozen chairs.

"You mind that feller they call the Gunsmith?"

"Clancy, you tellin' me that was him?"

"I am."

"The one they say is faster than grease lightnin'."

The man named Clancy turned back to the window, slipping the fingers of both hands deep into his hip pockets, his shoulders hunching some to accommodate the motion. He didn't answer the other's question. He simply sniffed, cleared his throat, and spat into the faded cuspidor near the cold jumbo stove in the center of the room.

"Arnold, you better go check with Skinner. He'll likely be hitting the saloons. Get three, four of the boys together, whoever's in town, and meet me back here." He paused, his eyes squinting now at the bare street outside the window.

"You sure, Clance?"

"Don't argue me, Arnold! Get yer ass movin'!"

"I meant, you sure it's really that Gunsmith feller?" Arnold was a lumpy man with a wide jaw that looked like a shovel. He had hands to match.

"There is a good way for you to find out, you dumb asshole. Now git! I want those men here right now. I'll check the Drovers to see if Casper's in town."

Big Arnold Oates was at the door. "Want me to send a rider for him if he ain't? He said somethin' about going down to Ten Fork."

Clancy seemed to hesitate, chopping off the answer that had sprung to his lips. "Naw. No. I'll see if he's in town, then we'll decide. *I* will decide," he added with emphasis, and his small round eyes were dark and hard on Oates, who, though for sure a good hand, needed some reining every now and again. Like just now.

He nodded as Oates went out, closing the door behind him. Then the foreman of the 88 Slash outfit took out his makings and began building himself a smoke.

He rode slowly down the main street of the small town, looking neither to right nor left, yet not missing a thing. He was taking it all in—the frame buildings, the boardwalks along each side of the street. Little wisps of dust lifted from Duke's hooves as he walked quietly toward where his rider knew the livery would be.

Heads turned to regard the stranger, but only one or two seemed interested enough to take a second look. He wondered if there were anyone to recognize him. And he wondered where the marshal's office might be.

It was the usual western town: a hotel, three eateries, some half-dozen saloons, a barber-bath, an undertaker, a blacksmith, a carpenter, a big general store, and two smaller shops that might be selling anything—it wasn't easy to tell from outside. And he knew there had to be a lawyer and maybe some land-office men. Yet the town, though shabby, had that look: that there was something afoot. Not trouble, necessarily, but action of some kind. The kind of action that would attract a lawyer, a businessman, a land-grabber, and the inevitable drummers. And there to his left was something that looked like it might be a newspaper office, and beside it a doctor's sign. And down there, he could see a couple of houses, set apart from the rest of the town: obviously cribs.

He drew rein at the hitching rack outside Cratchett's General Merchandise & Hardware Store. Dismounting, he wrapped his reins loosely around the single pole, using no knot that would impede a fast move out of town, if necessary. A flick of the wrist and the reins would be free. It was the next best thing to a horse knot, which too could be freed with a single pull.

For a moment he stood next to Duke, talking to him in a gentle and very quiet voice, telling him simply that he was going into the store to buy some ammo, and then they'd maybe take a look for the marshal's office.

The Gunsmith had spotted someone watching him as he rode past that first unpainted house at the edge of town, but he had no idea whether or not he'd been recognized. Could be it was someone just sizing the weather. But he could see right off that, quiet or not, Little Horn was a town where a lot of the doors swung both ways.

He still didn't see any sign marking the marshal's office, and he always made it a rule to check in with the law whenever he came into a town, especially a new place. It was a courtesy, after all. First of all, there was the fact that he'd been a lawman in the past; and then there was the unfortunate fact of his reputation. Clint Adams always made a point of covering himself regarding the law.

An older man with very narrow shoulders and big earlobes, wearing one suspender crosswise, greeted him.

"I am in need of ammo," Clint said, approaching the worn wooden counter.

The storekeeper's eyes flicked to the holstered .45. "Colt, huh?" His manner was friendly, he had unruly brown hair flying off in all directions, and his hands were thick, with liver spots on their backs.

"Two boxes," Clint said. "And two for the Winchester: .44-.40." He laid his money on the counter.

"Fine-looking hoss you got there," the storekeeper said.

Clint nodded. "I like him." He turned and started toward the door through which he'd entered, but then he stopped and turned back. "I'm looking for a man named Knox Hollinger. Know him, do you?"

The storekeeper looked like he wasn't ready for the question. He licked his thin lips, while his eyes darted to a table on which were stacked some bales of cloth. Then he pulled at one of his big earlobes. "Suggest you ask over to the marshal's office," he said. And he pointed to his left with a pretty stiff thumb.

Clint gave a nod to that but didn't say anything. Turning back to the door, he opened it and stepped outside. He was reaching back to close it when he felt the man behind him.

"If you're fixin' to stay in town there's the Drovers'. Any time; up the way there. Got good service, clean rooms, and the grub sticks to your ribs."

Clint almost grinned at that, but his face was straight as he asked, "Relation of yours run it?"

The storekeeper didn't bat an eye. "Fin Cole's my brother-in-law. Married my sister Ellie. My name's Chester Cratchett. Friends call me Dusty." A grin appeared suddenly in the form of a gap between two front teeth. "Tell 'em Dusty sent ya."

Clint nodded, a quiet smile on his face as he realized the man really wanted to be talking about something else.

"I will do that," he said. "I will tell them."

And as he walked down the boardwalk to the marshal's office, he wondered what it was that Dusty Cratchett had really wanted to talk about.

TWO

"Come fer the funeral, have yeh?" asked the twanging voice behind him.

He had stopped at the edge of the boardwalk just outside the marshal's office, having seen the sign said "Closed," and was pondering what to do next, his eyes sweeping the street down which he had just traveled.

Turning back now, he regarded the lounger squatting next to an empty crate just a few feet away from him. He wore a battered top hat that had once known grander days, though a piece had been chewed out of the brim and there was something that looked suspiciously like a hole both fore and aft. Yet its present owner wore it with regal indifference. Clint took him for a stove-up bronc stomper from some while back, too beat-up to handle a crowhopper let alone sunfishing on top of any green stuff. Likely, he did all his riding with his mouth around the saloon circuit; and he sure didn't look anything less than ornery. There was a glint in his eye now as he spat

9

down between the cracks of the boardwalk where he was
hunkered with his back holding up the marshal's office.

"Somebody important?" Clint said it casually, feeling
there was more in the oldster's remark.

The lounger's head moved slightly in the direction of the
door alongside him. "You lookin' for the marshal, are ya?"

"Mister, I asked you a question."

The bronc stomper came right together with that and
looked sharply at the stranger who had come to town.

"And I am tellin' you, mister, the marshal of this here
town is up to the cemetery. I am sayin', for good and all."

Something funny went through Clint Adams then—
a kind of wild current. And without any hesitation, and
somehow even knowing the answer, he asked, "What
name was he wearing? The marshal?"

The man who had been chewing pretty fast on his plug of
tobacco didn't appear to pause, even to spit, but said right
out, like it was part of his chewing, "Knox Hollinger.
An' some folks sayin' good riddance to bad rubbish."

Clint didn't pause either. "Who says that?"

Color flashed into the other man's face as he suddenly
found himself in a whole new conversation. But he
rallied, saying, "You knew him, did ya?" But his words
were pale, barely covering the acceleration of something
inside him.

Clint Adams stepped down off the boardwalk and
stood in the dirt street, looking right at the old lounger
who had suddenly stopped chewing.

"I *still* know him," he said.

The Drovers' Rest had been built little more than two
years before. It was said to be an almost exact replica of

its namesake in Laramie, though in smaller scale, Little Horn itself being also a good size smaller than the town that had inspired one of its renowned citizens to copy its hotel further north and west on the frontier.

The famous citizen who had left Laramie to contribute his unique talent towards bringing civilization to the land up near the Snake and Yellowstone rivers was not one who had forged the Great American West by fighting the Indian, the outlaw, and the weather, not to mention those duplicitous land speculators and other foes of the heroes of Manifest Destiny. Rather, he was a man deeply concerned with the circulation of the great wealth that was so obviously to hand in those exciting and sometimes perilous times.

And he favored his role as "a man of the people"; and as such his rather large photograph—taken, it was said, by the famous Mathew Brady—hung framed in full display in the lobby of the Drovers' Rest. The legend beneath it announced that this was Tennessee Fitzsimmons, "A man of, by, and for the People."

Another photograph, equally large, hung in the dining room. It showed Tennessee in the uniform of an army colonel at the time that he was in command of the Colorado militia just after the cessation of hostilities between the North and South.

Clint Adams had heard of Tennessee Fitz, as he was generally called, though it wouldn't have mattered if he hadn't. He had come north looking for Knox Hollinger, in answer to Knox's letter saying that things were getting pretty tight in Little Horn. The Gunsmith had known Knox well back in the days when he too had been a lawman, and he knew that things must be pretty bad indeed for such a capable party to send for help. Not that the letter had actually asked for help; but in Knox's droll fashion he had simply suggested that his old friend Clint might be "interested in a change of scenery, it being pretty hot around here right now."

The message was clear as his friend's signature, and as soon as he'd finished the letter Clint had stabled his team of bays and his gunsmithing wagon and saddled Duke. A very light rain had been falling as they'd headed north towards the Yellowstone.

Now, studying the pictures of Tennessee Fitz, first in the Drovers' lobby, then in the dining room, he decided to go back up to his room and catch up on some needed sleep. Also, he wanted to sort out his thoughts about the funeral and the people he'd seen there, especially why Tennessee Fitzsimmons, such an important person in Little Horn, had not attended services for the town marshal. But he was also very curious to know who was the good-looking young woman he'd seen standing with some older men and women. She'd seemed part of a group, yet she had an aura of separateness, as though she were a visitor in town.

It was hot in the little room one flight up. Clint drew the shade on the one window to keep out the sunlight, which was right at the sill; but it didn't help much. And so he stretched out flat on his back on the bed with the lumpy, cornhusk mattress on top of the twanging springs. While he did feel drowsy, he found that his thoughts were racing. For the moment at any rate, sleep was out of the question.

He had arrived at the cemetery just as the service was beginning. There had not been many people present.

The long, thin preacher had read the standard burial service quickly, and the gravediggers had fallen to closing
in the grave. Clint had been just as glad to have it
short: He was not a man who favored drawn-out fare-
wells.

At graveside he'd studied the mourners. He had right
off spotted Dusty Cratchett, who'd avoided his eyes;
then a tall man in a black frock coat who looked as
though he might own a good piece of the gambling in
town; an elderly couple; a middle-aged couple; two men
who might have been deputies, looking as though they
had nothing else to do but carry their sidearms around
town; and three important-looking men, with successful
paunches, heavy jowls, and greedy eyes, revealing the
prepared behavior of persons concerned with banking,
the legal profession, or simply the acquisition of riches
and power. And then there was the lone young woman
standing within the solemnity of the two couples. After
all, she was the best thing there, the best thing he'd seen
in a goodly while.

Knox, he remembered, had had no relatives, or at any
rate none that he'd admitted to. And so perhaps she was
a girlfriend, he'd thought. But he'd been in for a surprise,
for without any warning the gentleman now holding the
Good Book against his heart had all at once mentioned
Knox Hollinger's wife, Esther, who had died only some
months earlier of the croup, beside whom Knox was now
being laid to rest.

Unlike his wife, Knox Hollinger had not died of the
croup. The marshal of Little Horn had died from a bullet
between his shoulder blades. He had been shot in the
back. He had been murdered.

Clint Adams lay on his bed in the little room, quietly
turning it all over, feeling chastened that he'd not gotten
to Little Horn sooner, so that he could have helped his
friend. Still, he was a fatalist, and he realized that was
the way of it.

Somehow, he had not thought of Knox being married;
though why not? He was a good man. A damn good man.
He opened the letter again now and read it once more. It
was typical Knox: clean, short, and to the point. But it
contained no word of real worry and, unfortunately, no
names, no clue as to what the trouble had been.

Well, he had thought it through a couple of times,
and there was no gain in brooding over it. He didn't
have enough material to build any theory for why Knox
had been killed or who had done it. The obvious thing,
of course, was that the marshal of Little Horn had been
getting too close to somebody about something. Someone
had felt threatened and so had taken action. But more than
that . . . ?

Clint closed his eyes. It was warm, warmer than it had
been when he'd first come into the small room. And then,
all at once, he was wide awake, standing beside his bed
with his six-gun in his fist.

Again he heard the movement out in the corridor.

It was an extraordinary caravan. The wagons were
two-wheeled, following each other in single file, their
bright colors even more vivid in the dull morning light
that had followed the early rain. They were small wagons,
closed, sturdily built, with high wheels. Each showed
three glazed windows on either side, with double doors
at the front that opened onto a wide board, making a kind

of porch. The roofs were painted red, white, and blue, and they hung over the driver's seat, while the wooden sides were heavily varnished and painted like the roofs. Each wagon, though built along the same lines, was decorated differently, some having red window frames, others yellow or blue. Still others had designs painted on their varnished bodies. The big wheels were also paint-ed—red, green, or yellow. One wagon had yellow lines painted down the red spokes.

Still, they were wagons that had seen much in their time. As had the horses that pulled them. Then there were the cages bringing up the rear of the column. In the first one a tiger, looking rather moth-eaten, tried to pace back and forth as his cage bounced and twisted over the difficult trail. The next cage held half a dozen monkeys, and the last housed a grizzly bear.

With these strange vehicles were three orthodox Con-estoga wagons, in which people were obviously riding. Each was pulled by either horses or mules. And there were three men on horseback accompanying this inter-esting spectacle.

Yet that was not all. A few hundred yards behind the train of wagons, a cart, slowly drawn by a pair of mules, was proceeding along the same trail. This was an unpainted, battered, though sturdy, four-wheeled vehicle, with a driver's seat and end-gate. Every now and again, one of the three horsemen would drop back to exhort the driver to skin his mules faster so that they wouldn't keep falling behind, but this encouragement was of small avail. The mules—as mules do—made their own pace.

Their load was heavy. The wagon itself was big, built for rough travel, and loaded with barrels and crates. The whole load was covered with canvas, lashed to the body of the wagon. The barrels were filled with whiskey, and the crates with bottles of the same.

Two veterans of the frontier sat on the wagon box-seat directly behind the mules. A third man, equally honed by the vicissitudes of frontier life, rode beside them on an ancient gray mare with a sagging body. The rider now and again opined that it was easy riding, "like swinging in a hammock."

Overhead, the white disc that was the sun burned down on men and animals alike.

"I am layin' odds on a short spring," said the oldster holding the leather lines of the team pulling the heavy whiskey wagon. His beard, stained yellow with tobacco and spittle, quivered as he spat lazily onto the rump of one of the mules. "By the Great Horned Spoon, I could for sure use me a nip of that there whiskey!"

With each plodding step the mules bobbed their heads, but nobody even dreamed of trying to get them to move faster. These men were veterans; they knew their own limitations and the limits of their animals. The man seated next to the driver nodded as he dozed.

A rider a short way ahead of the wagon had turned his horse and was riding back. "Crick up yonder," he called. "Good place to let 'em blow. An' give us a rest."

"What about them-all?" The driver nodded his head toward the brightly colored wagons up ahead.

"They'll likely pull up too," the rider, whose name was Honey Mellody, said. He wore a tattered patch over one eye, where somebody's thumb had gouged him during a barroom scuffle.

The driver of the whiskey wagon, a grave-looking man

behind his rusty gray beard, flicked his lines over the rumps of his mules, who did not increase their plodding pace; though one of them circled one ear, and the other bared its teeth.

The three men—driver, companion, and Honey Mellody on his gray mare—approached the line of willows and cottonwoods that indicated the presence of a creek. They were all thirsty, as were their animals. As they reached the trees, they saw that the caravan ahead had already pulled up.

The driver of the whiskey wagon, Stinking Water Josh Hissinger, removed his wide black hat and ran a sleeved arm across his wet forehead.

"Hotter'n a bucket of piss ants in hell," he observed, drawing rein.

His companion on the box-seat—a man indifferent-ly bearing the name Grizzly Poland—rubbed the palms of his hands together. "I am looking forward to a little one about just that size," he said, holding his hands apart to measure about a foot of whiskey—or a bottle's contents, at any rate.

Moments later, in the shade now, Stinking Water brought forth a deck of cards. Grizzly opened the bottle he had kept for just that purpose and took the first swig, then passed it to Honey Mellody, who was to his left.

"Should always pass to yer right," Stinking Water said. "So I'll just take me a little extry to even it."

"Shit take it," Honey said, gasping as he lowered the bottle, his eyes russet-colored, his chin wet with whiskey.

"Honey," said Stinking Water, as he lifted the bottle, "our boys up ahead riding point—they got their eyes peeled for them heathen redskins, have they?"

"They do indeed," Honey said, his eyes glistening from the pleasure of the bottle that was being passed among the three.

Ensconced in the friendly shade, the three relaxed as they addressed themselves to jerked beef, canned peaches, and their own merchandise. And at the same time, they began to enjoy the pleasures of a game of chance with the deck that Stinking Water Josh had produced.

Presently, one head began to nod, then another, and finally even Honey Mellody, the youngest of the elderly trio, started to pop off.

He was suddenly brought wide awake with the clop of a horse's hooves racing in. It was Hank Henderson, one of the men riding flank, pulling up fast and shouting. "Get yer asses and the wagon up close! Smithers just rode back, sayin' there is Injuns up ahead round the butte." He pointed, his breath coming fast.

Honey was already scrambling to his feet. His two companions opened sleepy eyes. Then, suddenly catching the alarm as Henderson pounded off toward the other wagons, they were wildly sober.

"Let's cut them buggers," said Stinking Water. "Looks like the bunch ahead's heading for that tableland and the thickets. Mellody, you get up ahead there and find out from the Reverend where he wants us. Course, it could be just the Injuns that's buyin' this here merchandise," he added suddenly, on reflection.

"Don't sound like it," Grizzly said. "Not by the way Henderson was cuttin' his horse."

In moments they were on their way, Stinking Water

whipping and cussing the mules as he skinned them along the edges of the willow and cottonwoods.

Then another rider came pounding back to them.

"Who that!" Grizzly wanted to know, his beard quivering with excitement as he belched whiskey into the atmosphere.

"Jesus!" snapped Stinking Water. "You let fly like that at them redskins, they ain't gonna have the chance of a flea in hell!"

The rider was Coley Gallagher, coming up fast on a little dun pony with a wild look in its eyes. Drawing rein hard enough to throw up dust, Coley glared at the two men on the wagon seat. "Reverend says by God to git yer asses up there by them breaks, and pronto. Wants to know what the hell you bin doin' down here!" He sniffed. "Gimme a hit of that firewater, dammit!"

Reaching over, he grabbed the proffered bottle and took a swig, spluttering and coughing and almost dropping the precious fluid, but able to control himself. "By God, it puts a bullet in yer gun, don't it, boys!" With a wild grin, he turned the dun horse. "Git movin' or His Reverence will be jumping up yer ass, boys. He says somebody goddammit fucked up tellin' us there was no hostiles around."

"But maybe it's them 'Rapahoes what we were supposed to meet up with and it ain't hostiles," Stinking Water said again. "Shit, we don't want to shoot up our customers!"

And shortly, as it happened, Stinking Water Josh Hissinger, was proven partially correct. And he said so. "It warn't hostillies after all, and thank the good Lord for that, by God!"

It turned out to be three raunchy saddle bums loaded with firewater—internally—who'd taken the notion to hold up "the fancy wagon train with all them prettied-up colors"—just to have a little fun.

But the Reverend Crispus Quinn, who was guiding his flock to the promised land of milk, honey, and wealth, being wondrously perceptive in regard to other people's true, base motives, wasn't fooled by the initial friendly approach of the trio. And at the precise moment when their leader, a bucktoothed young man, decided to throw down on the Reverend and his retinue, the man who had anointed himself as leader of the people fired a round of blue whistlers from his handy shotgun, so close to the leader's head that the young fellow turned snow white and fainted right out of his saddle, falling into a pile of fresh horse manure.

"Where the sonofabitch belonged in the first place," intoned the Reverend as he lit a cigar.

In any case, it turned out that the three saddle bums were sent packing, minus their weapons, and the Reverend chose that moment to conduct a prayer of thanksgiving for the wagon train's swift deliverance from evil hands.

Shortly after the meeting, the three oldsters who had been bringing up the rear with the whiskey wagon found themselves in a fiery audience with the Reverend, who yet again had found it necessary to reprimand them on their less than useful behavior. "You're all slower than a bunch of drunk ants in a gluepot, fer Christ sakes!"

The Reverend Crispus Quinn was a whip-lean gentleman with a magnificent jaw, rather big ears lying close to his oblong head, which was thatched with gray hair, and a fierce goatee and tongue. He had long, spatulated fingers, which, when folded in prayer, gave the impression that indeed they had been born for just that purpose. And when they were curved around the butt of a .45, they seemed to say the very same thing. In truth, Crispus Quinn was a man of parts—a man of God, of the Devil, and many others in between. Those long fingers, stemming from those long, delicate-looking hands, could appear as flowers or talons. And Crisp Quinn, as he had been known back in his riverboat and traveling-theater days, was a born monger in many fields. Riverboat gambler, faro dealer, gunslinger, assayer of yellow wealth, he seemed able to identify with so many facets of the human character that some who had known him a little longer than usual asserted that he was like a chameleon. These observers were usually women, their company over longer periods of time being more acceptable than companions of the other gender. And the Reverend— that "great thespian of major caliber," as he saw himself—worked hard at the part, whatever it happened to be at a given moment.

For instance when he was through lecturing the whiskey trio, he returned to his private wagon and, disrobing, donned his "gun suit": black hat, black gloves, black boots and trousers, and tight black shirt. He no longer appeared slow, thoughtful, holy.

Riding point now, and feeling good about the way he had dressed down those three drunken louts who were skinning the whiskey wagon, as well as the way he had backwatered those drunken saddle bums, the Reverend, as he was called by everyone, felt on top of the world.

As he rode now—the "Great Scout of the West-

ern Frontier"—his hand brushed his sidearm, and he
realized that he had forgotten to reload the shotgun,
which was in its scabbard by his knee. Damn! He
had better watch that. Likely no one had noticed this
breach in gunslinging care and maintenance. Nor, surely,
did anyone share his sudden secret: The "Avenging
Angel," the "Black Ace," had in point of fact missed
his target, even with that scatter gun. For he had not
aimed to frighten that young bucktoothed hoodlum but
to kill him.

THREE

The girl was young and pretty, yet with a sheen that she wore like a light suit of armor as she stepped into the room. Her eyes were mostly on the gun that Clint Adams was holding.

"I was just about to knock," she said.

"That is what I figured."

"Is that thing your usual greeting card with company?" She had red hair and green eyes. A calico dress of blue and white encased a figure that understood there was no such thing as a straight line between two points.

"Depends on the company," he said, slipping the .45 back into its holster. Reaching over with his foot, he pushed the door shut.

"I am alone," she said.

"I know."

"I see you're a man who's got his life right where he wants it, Mister, uh . . ."

"Adams. Clint Adams."

"My name's Kelly. Kelly O'Shay."

"So what can I do for you?"

She gave a little shrug with her face and hands. "I'd figured it was a question of what I could do for you, sir."

Clint had an awfully strong impulse to laugh, but he checked it. He still had part of his attention on the corridor outside. And on the window, too. At the same time, there was no getting out of the fact that the girl was special. That good-looking, and putting it on the line like that! It was something to wonder about. But not for too long. The Gunsmith had learned long before never to let his surprise or personal, physical interest in anyone steal his attention.

She was standing very still with her hands together at her waist; and now she dropped her eyes. He was suddenly aware that one of her legs was trembling. But before he could speak she looked up, and he saw the tears standing in her eyes. Yet she had hold of herself.

"I don't want to do this," she said suddenly in a new voice. "I don't . . . I don't . . . I can't . . ." All at once she tossed her head, biting her lip.

"Who put you up to it?"

She looked down at her hands, shaking her head.

"Tell me straight," he said. "Somebody put you up to setting me up."

She was looking at him now, and she had control of herself. "Look, mister, I don't know you. But . . . but I don't want to be a part of something like this."

"Who is it?"

"I don't know their names. But they, well, they

made me do it. Except, I can't. I'm not that hard up!
Dammit!"

"What were they planning to do?"

"Beat you up, I think. At least from the way they
were talking. But I don't know for sure. Maybe—
maybe worse. I don't know. They wanted you, like off
guard."

"It's an old game," he said. "So when are they supposed to come?"

"They didn't say. They just told me to—to soften
you up. Get your guard down, I guess is what they
meant."

"Well, at least I have to say that, whoever they are,
they've got good taste."

But she didn't pick that up. He judged it as telling him
something in her favor. While they had been talking, he
had buckled on his gunbelt.

"Judging the time," he said then, "you've been here
maybe ten minutes. They'd be figuring on maybe twenty
or a half-hour, for sure. What do you think?"

"I don't know. I'm not an expert in this field."

He could see now that she had control of herself again.
"But what do you do for a living?" he asked.

Her cheeks had reddened. "I, well, I had been hoping
to start a new career. Since my business, my store . . .
well, since business is so bad. Or, well, Millie and
myself—she's my sister—we just ran out of money.
And we decided we had to do something because we were
really and truly desperate. We tossed a coin for it, and
I . . ."

"Lost? Won? Which?"

She gave a small, wan smile as she shrugged.

"So I've been trying to start a new—career, I suppose I could say. We owe a lot of money."

He stared at her and realized that his jaw had dropped. "Do you mean to tell me that you suddenly up and decided that you were going to be a . . . a . . ."

"A whore," she said calmly. "Why, yes. You see, Millie isn't well. And anyway, I lost when we tossed the coin. And so I went to this place and inquired, and—"

It was just at this point that Clint heard a scuffing sound on the other side of the door, and he made a motion to her to be quiet.

The door was locked; yet there was also the window. Quickly, he stepped over to a position from which he could look outside without being seen. There was no balcony, as he already knew. Nobody could come in from that direction, except with a ladder; but there was none. Then it had to be only the door; not a two-way attack.

He knew it was one of the oldest tricks in that big bundle of old tricks. Get a man with his pants down and then clobber him. What was surprising to him was the girl. She didn't look like the usual bird. She didn't talk like it, and he was willing to bet she didn't make love like it. Then he spotted the edge of white paper under the door.

The girl was standing in the corner of the room on the far side of the bed. With his knife he fished the paper through, keeping himself as much away from the door as possible.

The message was simple: "Friend, the girl is a gift. Take it and get out of town. There is only one problem here. You." It was unsigned.

He looked at the girl. "What are you going to tell them when you go back?" he asked.

"I'm not going back." She was much tighter now than she had been. It seemed she had worked herself up into the job she had to do, but now there wasn't that much left for her to improvise. Yet he could see that she had her courage. He felt touched and suddenly, in a strange way, drawn to her; drawn apart from the fact that she was damn good-looking.

He handed her the note.

She seemed to scan it and then read it over. She handed it back to him.

"Why didn't they come in?" he asked.

"I was supposed to call out. You know, like I was having a good time."

"What will you do when they find out?"

"I don't know. I'll have to think of something." She had come around to his side of the bed now. "I am sorry. I just got all rattled with money troubles and with Millie and all. But that's nothing to do with you."

He wondered about Millie but didn't ask. "Go carefully," he said.

She was standing in the middle of the room, facing him. "And you," she said.

And then she was gone.

He waited until he figured she'd reached the lobby, then he quietly opened the door, checked the corridor, and slipped out. There was a window at the end of the hall that looked out onto Main Street. It gave him a good view of the street in front of the Drovers' Rest.

And there she was. He watched her walk out of sight. Nobody appeared to be following her. When he came down to the lobby, there was only an old man, sitting in an armchair reading a newspaper, and the room clerk in back of the desk, who didn't give any indication that he had noticed him.

And so it was an interesting play. It told him something about who was running it. First, he was known as a threat. Second, for the present they only wanted to scare him off. Yes, it was an old trick they'd tried to pull. But it had a new wrinkle. And it was this that struck him. Whoever was running the show had picked a new girl for the job—an innocent? It showed Clint Adams that whoever it was, it was a person with imagination, if not an interesting sense of humor, as well as a fair judge of character.

He had chosen to ride out early, before most of Little Horn was up, and he had picked a good moment. The first sunlight was just washing the tips of the distant mountains as he rode Duke out to the small cemetery. Knox's grave was still fresh from the day before; he was lying alongside his wife, Esther, near some juniper bushes. The markers were alike—simple. Name and date. He wondered who had taken care of his friend's affairs.

He stood there wondering how Knox had been in the years since he'd last seen him. And he wondered too what sort of woman Esther had been.

He realized suddenly that he had taken his hat off, and he berated himself for his lack of attention. Maybe that was what had happened to Knox: His attention, his sharpness and his instinctive awareness, had failed him momentarily. Had he died right away? To be shot in the back! Was there a moment when he had *known*? Before it happened?

Someone had brought some more flowers since the day before. And as he looked at them, wondering who had brought them, he knew that somebody was near.

He had a good notion who it was even before he turned and saw her.

"Mr. Adams? I am Norah Caldwell. Knox described you to me. I—I hope you are Mr. Adams."

And her sudden alarm that he might not be was so delightful he burst out laughing.

"Yes, I'm still Clint Adams," he said. "Was it you who put these flowers?"

"Yes, it was. I did it after everyone had left." She looked down and then directly at him. "I'm afraid I just don't like funerals very much. And yesterday . . ."

"The atmosphere was too funereal, wasn't it?" he said. "For me, I know Knox wouldn't have put up with it. Likely he'd have let out a whoop and started something wild to wake everybody up."

They both laughed at that.

She was wearing a different outfit now, a superb riding habit, which told him she took pains with her appearance. She was of average height, with dark brown hair, dark brown eyes, and a figure that set off her pearl-gray blouse and black britches in an alarmingly exciting manner. Yet her movements were not provocative. And he realized that her quality was such that she didn't need to provoke, excite, or titillate. All she had to do was be wherever she happened to be.

"I take it, then, you're Knox's friend, though he didn't mention you in his letter to me."

"I know. He told me he was writing to you. I'm so glad you could come." And he saw something flick into her eyes.

Then she said simply, but with not a trace of self-pity, "There hasn't been anybody to talk to about . . . things."

They had begun to walk toward the town, and Clint realized it was still early, for a number of people were not yet about. A dog barked as they entered Main Street, and the barber opened the door of his shop, ready for business.

"Have you eaten yet?" he asked.

"I'd love some coffee. I stayed in town last night, and I should be getting back to—back home soon."

They had arrived at the O.K. Cafe, which had evidently just opened, judging by the sighing and muttering of the gentleman in charge of the kitchen. Upon entering, they had chosen a small table by a window, and he emerged scowling, scratching his arm and sighing with angry self-pity, as though he were carrying the load of the world.

"What'll it be?"

"Just coffee," Norah said.

"Likewise."

It was the proprietor waiting on them, Clint could tell, for he kept looking toward the door as though expecting his hired help to arrive, which was obviously late. Sure enough, the door opened and a young woman hurried in and disappeared into the kitchen, from which there shortly came a loud and severe round of scolding.

Presently the girl emerged with their coffee in steaming mugs. "Anything else?" she asked. She was a large girl and looked well able to take care of herself, but Clint could see she was on the edge of a severe attack of the giggles.

"You always come late!" came the angry voice from the kitchen.

"It's because you work me too hard," the girl called back, winking at Clint and the girl.

Clint grinned at her. "Tell him to go sit on a tack," he said.

"Go sit on a tack!" the girl shouted suddenly. And then, turning to Clint, she said, "That's what the kids say at school all the time."

Meanwhile, the proprietor had appeared in the doorway into the kitchen. "Ah! I see you engage the customers in your frivolities! Hah! A fine thing, talking to the customers behind my back! Now, get in here!" He wagged his thumb over his shoulder several times, indicating that she get to work instantly.

Suddenly the girl was different. She became soft, fluid; she even seemed to lose some of her great weight. "Ah, caro mio! I will do anything you ask. Command me! Emile! Oh, Master!" And she all but flowed across the floor into the kitchen, giving Emile such a sensuous stroke along his big belly it would have brought a buffalo into subservience.

Neither Clint nor Norah could hold their laughter any longer.

But Emile was still grumbling as he followed the girl, though directing his barrage toward his customers. "You see, the sort of help I get! I, who have to do all the hard work around this place! And I am treated in this terrible fashion!"

But now from the kitchen came abrupt silence.

The Gunsmith did hear something in a moment, though he wasn't quite sure what it was. "Let's go," he said. "We'll get coffee someplace else." Without waiting for Norah to respond, he stood up, put some money on the table, and led her swiftly to the door.

When they were outside she asked, "Why? What happened? Was something wrong?"

"I don't know. I just had a feeling, and also I heard something in the kitchen."

"But it could have been a cook or somebody."

"Yes, it could. But I don't think it was."

"Do you think it was someone interested in our talking about Knox?"

"Maybe. It was more a feeling than anything else."

"And you're a man who listens to his feelings," she said as they arrived at the livery.

"Sure I do."

"Like Knox." He looked at her, catching the sadness in her voice.

"You loved him?" Clint asked.

"Knox was my best friend."

He was glad they had the saddling and bridling to attend to now, for he saw that she needed action, not words. And not memories.

Mostly they rode in silence. Norah explained to him how she had taken care of Knox's effects after he had been killed. He'd had no relatives, and she had long been a friend of both Knox and Esther.

They reached the top of a long draw around noontime and were able to look down on the R Bar O, where Knox had run about 250 head of cattle. The heat was heavy on the land, and Clint felt the sweat down his back as they sat their horses and looked down on the log cabin, the barn, horse corral, and a couple of sheds.

"Knox told me the 88 Slash was using this as a line camp some years back, but then they just let it go on account of running their stock farther east and north. It was deserted for a good while, and then Knox bought it."

"I see." Clint was studying the place through his field glasses.

"But then Casper decided the 88 could use this grazing and the place as a line camp again, and he tried to buy it back from Knox."

"Who refused to sell," said Clint with a tight grin, knowing very well how his friend would have taken such a proposal.

"Who refused to sell," Norah repeated, keeping her eyes on the buildings below.

"And that's what did it."

She nodded. "They started cutting his fences, rustling his stock, and a whole lot of things. All the time, Casper used to ride over to see Knox and smile and make an offer. All smarmy like."

"Oh yes, I know how that is."

"My dad used to have his outfit the other side of that butte," she said suddenly.

"*Used* to?"

"He was one of the 88's cowboys. Tried to make it. Well, it was all right while he was still alive, but then, well, it was left to me and my brother, Tom. We still use the place. Casper lets us stay there, but we've had to borrow so much money through the bank that they as good as own it."

"Your brother is there now?"

She nodded. "He manages the place. But he's not very happy about it." Then she added, "Nor am I."

"I wouldn't be either," Clint said.

He was studying the layout below. He didn't see any horses about and none in the corral. In fact, he saw no livestock at all—not even a dog.

He was very much aware of the girl beside him, and he had been all during the ride out from Little Horn. Aware of his desire for her and at the same time aware of her sorrow over Knox.

"Nobody down there now, is there." He said it more as a statement than a question.

"Shouldn't be."

Of course, he was thinking, there could be a horse in the barn. He loosened the .45 in its holster and then started Duke down toward the ranch, quartering down the draw, in full view, with Norah following on her little bay horse.

He rode right up to the barn, and dismounted on the side away from the house. The girl followed suit.

"You stay out here," he said.

"What's the matter? You think somebody's here?"

"Maybe. You stay here, while I take a look in the barn."

But there was no one there. No horse, either. He stood still, listening. Only the sound of a pack rat scurrying somewhere. When he came out, Norah was waiting beside her horse.

"You still want me to stay here?"

He didn't answer right away. He was looking at the ground right in front of him. "You have any other horses?"

"The stock's all over with Tom at Elder Creek. Horses and cows, too."

Clint Adams had a notion, and he could feel it in his blood, his nerves, all through his body. He lifted his chin and looked at the sky. "How long ago did you run the stock over to your brother?"

"The day before yesterday."

"And you left here yesterday, did you?"

"Right. But something's wrong!"

"You feel it?"

"I don't know. But the way you're acting."

"Let's go in," he said, nodding toward the house.

"Of course," she said. "I can make that cup of coffee we never had in town."

He didn't let her enter first. Instead, he kept beside the doorway as he pushed, then kicked the door open. There was nobody there. The rooms were empty.

"Phew!" Norah sat down with a big sigh on the horsehair sofa and smiled fondly at him. "That's a relief, I must say. I'm going to make a cup of coffee."

But she could see he still wasn't satisfied.

"Just want to take another look. I'll be right back," he said.

Outside, he walked toward the corral, studying the ground as he went. At the corral, he also studied the ground but found nothing that was useful. He stood now just outside the corral, trying to come nearer to himself.

The sun was close to the horizon now and there was a change in the air. He could feel the heat leaving, but there was still plenty of light. He could see the rim of the trees at the top of the long draw. Then he looked at the log house again, thinking for an instant of Knox living there with his wife. And then with Norah? It wasn't his business.

And then all at once he realized just what he had been looking at and not really seeing.

The sun was right at the horizon now, and it wouldn't be long before nightfall.

The Gunsmith let all the breath out of his body, as his eyes softened and yet at the same time his sight sharpened. But there was no tension in them that wasn't needed. His hands hung easy at his sides as he started forward. He was looking directly at the outhouse just on the side of the barn, out of view of the house.

"Come on out with your hands up, mister! And right now!"

There was a beat, another beat; and then the door opened slowly and a man stepped out. He was wearing a holstered six-gun at his hip, but his hands were empty, away from his sides. He was ready to draw, Clint saw.

"How long you been in there?"

"Dunno. Maybe couple hours. More maybe." He was a chunky individual with a very red, wet-looking face, a farmer's wide-brimmed hat, galluses, and clodhopper boots. Clint realized he'd been drinking.

"What are you doing here?"

"Just come to court. Not that it's any your business. What the hell you think you're doin' here! Tryin' to cut me out? Well, you have made the biggest mistake in your life!"

His big red hand struck for his gun.

The Gunsmith didn't wait for his adversary to clear leather. Before that red-faced sodbuster had even touched the stock of his pistol, the Gunsmith had him covered.

"Freeze!"

He did. But he was also starting to shake.

"Who sent you here?"

"Nobody. I come on my own."

"Where's your horse?"

"Don't have one."

"Then how did you get here? Come on, I want answers!"

"My friend rode me over. From the other side of the tableland. He left me; had to go somewheres."

"And . . .?"

"He'd be comin' back for me."

"When?"

Just then Clint heard Duke nicker. He stepped around the man he was holding under his gun. The horse and rider were coming in from the other side of the cabin. Reaching out, Clint pulled the six-gun out of his prisoner's holster, and at that moment he saw two riders canter in. The Gunsmith had them well covered.

These two were not clodhoppers, however. It took only a split second to judge the caliber of the two lean gunswifts who pulled up in front of Clint and his prisoner.

"Fucked up again, huh, Lolly?" sneered the one on the blaze-faced bay.

"Man caught him with his pants down!" His companion, a man equally lean, riding a dun horse, laughed.

"Keep your hands out," Clint snapped, when the man on the bay moved.

"Don't worry, Gunsmith. We know who we're talking to, and we'll just wait till the odds are a little more even. Don't get your water steamed up."

"Take this feller and git!" Clint said, hard as the look that was holding them. "I don't want to see any of you around this place. Get out of here!" And he gave the man named Lolly a shove.

"No need to be unfriendly, Mr. Gunsmith," said the one on the dun. "We got a invite for you."

"From Mr. Casper," his companion said.

"I don't know him."

"He knows you," the first speaker said. "And he wants to see you. We was sent to get you."

"But your pal buggered it."

"We can still take you," said the one on the dun.

"Jake . . ." His companion lifted both his hands to make sure the Gunsmith knew he wasn't a part of such bravado.

"Chicken guts!" Jake sneered at his sidekick. He shrugged.

"Well, Gunsmith, we'll give Mr. Casper your message." He nodded to Lolly. "C'mon. Get up behind Chuck there."

The Gunsmith was watching Jake's hands as he put his reins against the dun's neck to turn him. One hand was holding the leather, the other was out of sight.

"Hold it!" The Gunsmith had them both covered with Lolly's gun. "Turn real slow, and drop the belly gun!"

As the hideout fell to the ground, Clint said, "You are lucky. Just remember this, and tell whatever his name is—Jasper-Casper—the straight of it. Now cut leather!"

"Mister . . ." It was Lolly, his mouth loose, wet,

his big eyes rolling. "We wuz only bringing a message. . . ."

"Now you're taking one. Git!" He made a slight movement with the Colt.

They cut leather.

FOUR

The girl cooked up some supper while he had coffee. Then, while they sat at the table and ate, she told him about Knox and the ranch and his trouble with the 88 Slash.

"I heard somebody say in town that this was going to be an 88 line camp again," Clint said. "Was that just rumor?"

"Whatever; it isn't the case," she said firmly. "Mr. Casper had been trying to buy out Knox and Knox wouldn't. So maybe he thinks that now he can somehow. Like I told you."

"But who owns the outfit now? Knox didn't have any relatives, did he?"

"He left the R Bar O to me."

"That seems like a good notion," Clint said.

"Yes . . ." She looked at him with her eyebrows raised and tightened her lips.

Clint Adams thought she had superb eyebrows;

41

indeed, superb everything. But he forced himself to stay with the business at hand.

She gave him an overview of what had been going on in and around Little Horn, which he had more or less figured out already; but hearing it from her gave it a dimension that was useful—the dimension of someone who had actually gone through some of it.

"So it's cut-and-dried as far as this feller Casper sees it? That's the way of it?"

She nodded. "And it's cut-and-dried the way Norah Caldwell sees it."

He grinned at her. "You know, I figured that's about what you'd say."

They both laughed at that.

"I have tried to get some hands to round up the stock."

"But they're all afraid of Casper," Clint said, filling in.

"They're all afraid of Casper."

He had already told her about his encounter with Casper's men and the invitation he'd received.

"If you don't mind," he said now, "I'd like to invite myself to spend the night. Those fellers might decide to come back."

She was already nodding her head. "Please. I want you to stay. I was going to ask you."

"Fact, I think you'd better think about moving into town," he said. "Or anyway, back to your own outfit. Though you say Casper wants that, too."

"The range butts together down by Rabbit Creek. So he wants the whole lot, of course."

Together they did the dishes. He'd built up the fire

in the kitchen range and then heated water in the galvanized tub.

Finally he said, "Better get some sleep."

She seemed to be thinking about something, and he said again, "You better get some sleep."

"What are you going to do?"

"Sleep."

"But tomorrow. What will you do tomorrow? I can help you check the cattle, over at our place."

"We'll see," he said. "We'll 'tend to tomorrow when it comes."

He caught the little smile on her face.

She offered him the bed in the extra room, but he told her he would bed down right in the kitchen.

"But that's a good bed in there. Why not sleep in it? Wouldn't you be more comfortable?"

"I reckon I would."

"Well, why not then?"

"I don't want to sleep comfortable," he said. "See, I could maybe sleep a whole lot longer than I want to."

"Oh . . ." And she gave a little laugh, but it was without humor. Then she just stood there looking at him. "I like the way you express yourself, Mr. Adams. I like the way you say things. And . . . and thank you." She ducked her head a little then and turned away.

"Call me Clint."

She turned back at the door of her bedroom. "Only if you call me Norah."

"Agreed."

He had the great urge then to just walk over and take her in his arms, but he knew it would be foolhardy. He remained where he was, while she stood in her doorway, looking at him.

"I'm not afraid of them coming back as long as you're here," she said.

"That is exactly why I have to stay awake." Then he added, "I can still rest—I know how from the trail. But I want you to get a good sleep. We've got a lot of work in the morning."

"Thank you," she said softly. "Clint."

When she had gone into her room, he unrolled the blanket he'd brought with him and added some bedding she'd left for him, then blew out the lamp and lay down.

After a few moments he got up, slipped outside, and took a turn around the buildings and corral, checking the outhouse, too. It was a clear night with a lot of stars, but he saw no sign of any unwanted visitors.

When he came back into the house he waited a moment or two, then moved his bed from the kitchen into the front room. He lay down fully clothed, his six-gun within easy reach. He lay there listening, turning over all that had taken place since he'd come to Little Horn. He thought of Knox and what had happened to him. And now and again he thought of the girl in the next room.

During the night the wind had risen. It was still dark when Clint awoke. He had slept lightly, the way he always did on the trail, and now he was fully awake. He lay on his bedding, listening. The only sounds he heard were in the house: a window rattling, a pack rat exploring the foundation.

Now the rain. Soft. He waited, listening to his body, himself; feeling the day, the atmosphere around him. He liked to awaken like that: to come into the day smoothly through the contact with the life of his body; in that way he had himself. Which was all he really needed: himself.

He got up and rolled his bedding, hearing the girl begin moving in her room at the same time that he stirred. It was as though she had been waiting. Then she came out, smiling a good morning at him, and walked into the kitchen. In a few moments she had built a fire and was boiling up some coffee.

"Any extra armaments around here?" he asked.

"You mean a gun?"

"Should be something of Knox's about."

She led him to the other bedroom and opened a large trunk and removed a bunch of old clothes that were nevertheless folded, revealing a variety of guns that had obviously belonged to Knox Hollinger.

"Take your pick. They should be in good working condition. Knox always took care of his guns. And his horses," she added.

He picked up a wicked-looking scattergun. Then he asked her about horses.

"About six head down by the breaks," she told him. "I wouldn't have thought you'd be needing a horse with that beautiful black you've got."

"Just wanted to check on the stock."

"Sure. Well, I told you Knox's last cattle tally was 250 head, give or take."

"And that's it?"

"There's Roscoe. He used to be a first-class shepherd dog; could wrangle cattle, too. Tough. But, he's long in the tooth and stove up, from a horse kicking him."

"He thought he could wrangle horses, did he?" Clint said with a grin. "Well, old Roscoe was nowhere to be seen when I was snooping about."

"I didn't know you were a snoop."

All of a sudden her attitude had shifted. It was slight, and if he had been less keen he wouldn't have noticed. But the playfulness was surely there.

"When I was seeing the outfit was buttoned down for the night," he said. "By the bye, how did you sleep?"

She looked down at her hands. "Not very well," she said. She looked at him then. "How did you?"

"Not very well."

Her eyes went to the window. "It's still dark. Still nighttime outside."

"And in here the same."

There followed a long pause, while they heard the coffee boiling. Suddenly it sounded as though it would boil over, and they both ran to the kitchen.

"Like a cup?" she asked as he came up behind her.

"No." Then: "Would you?"

"No."

She had turned and was looking directly at his chin.

He said, "I don't feel like coffee, even though I bet you made a great cup."

She lifted her head then and their eyes met. In the next moment, he had his arms around her.

The thought that her lips were soft as the dawn swept through his mind; and her kiss was warm as the sun.

His erection had been instanteous, and her legs parted beneath her dress to receive it.

Then he picked her up as she held him around his neck and he carried her into the bedroom.

They didn't hurry. They took their time. He liked that a lot. She had a beautiful body, which he had known all along.

"You've a beautiful body," she said to him. "I am so glad." Standing beside him, the two of them naked now, she ran her hands over his chest.

"You too," he said, caressing her high breasts. Bending slightly, he took one of them in his mouth, while one hand reached down to explore her great bush of dark brown hair.

Meanwhile, she had both hands on his erection and was slowly stroking it to his utter delight, her fist sliding along the long, thick shaft.

"I want him in my mouth," she said. "May I?"

"You can do anything you like with him," he said. "That's what he's for."

And she was kissing it, licking it, sucking it in deep, slow strokes. All the while he thought he would lose his mind totally. Seated on the edge of the bed, she had spread her legs and was sucking furiously, while he reached his hands down for each breast, stroking and squeezing. Then he held her head as it bobbed up and down on his member, taking long, soaking strokes that brought him to the most exquisite joy.

"I want you inside," she said.

Clint was obliging. She lay on her back with her knees up, spread wide for his entry. He entered, his member at its hardest, longest, thickest. Slowly, gently, he stroked her as she began to moan, her hands gripping his pumping buttocks, then reaching down to fondle his balls. Hugging each other, together they increased their tempo, while their breath mingled and accelerated. Finally, neither could hold it any longer, and in a racing crescendo they came together.

"My God!" she gasped. "My God!" Her thighs gripped him, and her hands stroked his back, his buttocks, while they kept coming until the last, exquisite drop.

Seldom did Elijah Robert Fitzsimmons pass through the lobby or dining room of the Drovers' Rest without cutting at least a surreptitious glance at one or both likenesses of himself revealed so boldly and in such glorious detail. The present moment was no exception, and since the lobby was for the moment deserted, he took a longer look at the figure in the gilt frame overlooking the arrival and departure of the various guests.

A few moments later, he found himself in front of his heavily uniformed self in command of the Colorado militia. Strangely, Tennessee was never known to be explicit about his actual military activities. Whenever questioned by enthusiasts, he tended to look off in another direction, slightly embarrassed, rather scouting the whole affair and even remarking at times that whatever one might have heard of his exploits was grossly exaggerated.

All of which supported the picture of an honest, modest man who—when assisted by the inevitable passage of time— would eventually acquire the honored patina of a "War Hero."

He was standing now in the doorway to the billiard room, an unlit cigar in his hand, a pensive look in both his dark eyes. Tennessee Fitz was deciding how he would meet with the man whom he had kept waiting now for nearly half an hour. At last, having gone over his plan yet again and satisfied himself that his "game" would by now be at the point of fuming, he squared his round shoulders, sucked in his belly, and, clasping his hands behind him while still holding the cigar, raised himself up on his toes, and down, then up and down again. Finally, jutting out his chin, he marched down the length of the billiard room to the narrow door at the end. Opening it, he entered.

"Good evening," he said amiably to the man who was seated at the other side of the round card table. At the same time, he spoke over his shoulder to the waiter who had followed him in.

"See what Mr. Casper wants, and I'll have my usual." Nodding to the obviously angry man seated on the other side of the table, he seated himself carefully, with a grand sigh. Then he bit off the little bullet of tobacco at the end of his cigar and lit it.

Then—obviously having forgotten—he seemed to suddenly remember and he offered a cigar to his guest.

Tennessee enjoyed watching the biggest rancher in that part of the territory fight down his impulse to refuse. He just happened to know—that is, he'd made it his business to find out—that Chance Casper enjoyed few things more than a good cigar.

Victorious in his maneuver, he could afford now to dispense largesse and so he leaned forward with a light for the tough old boy he had so neatly skewered.

"You wanted to see me, Casper?"

"You know I did, Tennessee. Just as you knew I would when your bank called my note."

"*My* bank!" Tennessee Fitz's big eyebrows shot up. "I surely wish it were my bank, friend!"

But Chance Casper was no dummy, and he was as tough as everybody said. His face was as though carved from iron as he regarded the short, bulky man across the table. "You may not actually own the bank, Tennessee, but you damn near own every bit of paper and metal that goes across them counters. Don't hand me that poorhouse shit!"

But that was as far as he could push it. Casper knew it, but he was bullheaded and always had been—a man who had to say it and play it just like it lay. Yet he saw that was the line over which there would be no stepping.

"I think that's what we can call your opinion, sir," Tennessee said calmly. "And you are welcome to it. Now then, here are the conditions I am offering you for an extension on your rather generous loan, sir!"

The tone, delivered from the thin mouth under the cold, marble eyes, lowered the temperature in the room by several degrees.

Chance Casper leaned forward as Tennessee Fitz-simmons pushed the paper across the table. Pulling the single sheet toward him with his thick forefinger, he kept his hard eyes on the other man as he said, "This could just as easy bin done through Binns."

"I prefer not to deal with lawyers when possible," Tennessee said. "I invariably deal with principals; and this time is no exception."

"You like to see your fish fightin' the hook, huh?"

"If that's the way you look at it." The reply was quiet, without a trace of anger. "Look that over and, if you wish, sign it. If you don't, then don't." He stood up and started for the door.

Chance Casper stood up and began folding the paper as he watched the man who owned just about everything in town go out the door.

With his eyes on the empty door frame, he said quietly, "You sonofabitch."

Then Tennessee Fitzsimmons was back in the doorway. "I heard that, Casper, by damn! I heard that!"

"By God, you were meant to hear it!"

The Great Caravan of Mystery had finally come to a stop in the shadow of the high rimrocks that overlooked the town. The wagons were set in a semicircle, and the men of the traveling troupe had built corrals for the animals that had been domesticated—that is, the horses and mules. Those members of the caravan that were supposedly untamed—the tiger, the monkeys, the grizzly, and the snakes—remained caged in their usual quarters. This, the caravan's leader, the Reverend Crispus Quinn, had pointed out, enhanced their appeal to the public. Loose, those wild beings would not have carried the attraction they did when incarcerated. Behind bars, they were infinitely more "dangerous" than wandering around loose. The exception was Ralph, the "Great Man-Eating Grizzly," who was in fact all but toothless and also slightly moth-eaten as to fur. The frequent companion of his mentor, Grizzly Poland, Grizzly and Ralph had created a pretty big stir when they appeared on Little Horn's main street that first afternoon, Ralph with a poster attached to his back announcing the carnival in rousing terms.

The townspeople had turned out in large numbers to visit the big excitement. The brightly colored wagons, carefully arranged in a horseshoe shape, seemed to draw the visitors like a magnet. No one had ever seen wagons quite like these. The area between the two prongs of this "magnet" was jammed. The women of the carnival, dressed in colorful, voluminous skirts and loose blouses, had started some cookfires, which some of the smaller children were fanning. The flames were shooting skyward in big, exciting spurts, at the same time licking the heavy iron pots that were supported by tripods. From the black cauldrons, delicious smells ascended into the sky and surrounding area, exciting the visitors, who soon started buying the delicacies.

Nearby, in the lee of a van that was covered by a tight canvas, several women were plucking chickens and talking merrily. Some children near them were rolling hoops, while others simply gaped at the townfolk, who gaped back. There were several dogs running about.

Now the women at the cookfires began serving the hot food to the children and some of the men. And at the same time, they offered food for sale to the crowd that had gathered.

Across from the fires ticket sellers had taken their places, and those of the crowd who wished could enter the roped-off area where the more curious could go right up to the cages of the tiger, the monkeys, the snakes, and also Ralph the grizzly, who was resting after having taken a walk with his master. Ropes had been arranged so that to get close to the cages, the customer had to pay at an admittance booth. It was all very orderly.

At one of the caravans there was a sign announcing that "Stella Will Tell Your Fortune with the Cards! Minerva Will Read the Crystal Ball!" Another wagon announced lessons in "Magic, Reading Palms, Reading a Person's Head!" and a third wagon had a ' banner on it stating that "The Ancient Tarot Cards Can Tell All—When Read by a Master!"

On the side of one of the wagons, a sign announced that there would be a shooting competition at an unannounced date; meanwhile, individuals could shoot for prizes at the target area.

Clint Adams had taken most of this in during a half-hour stroll, during which time he found a number of people looking at him. News had obviously gotten about that he was a friend of Knox Hollinger, and while no one spoke to him on the subject, he realized that a number of people had to be aware of what had taken place out at Knox's ranch. Of course, such news as the backwatering of Chance Casper's men would not only greatly interest the newsmongers in the various drinking places and sporting cribs, but it would also furnish endless speculation regarding what the next stage of the building drama would be.

Clint had noticed two groups of three or four men watching him: evidently riders or saddle toughs with Casper's outfit. So he was well on his guard and, as a result, he was glad he hadn't brought Norah with him.

He had ridden into town to check on the status of Knox's ranch with a lawyer Norah had told him about, and then he'd planned to ride out and confront Casper. But the caravan had prompted the notion that he might pick up some useful gossip that could help fill out his picture of the situation confronting him.

Then to his sudden astonishment, he saw the girl from the Drovers' Rest: the red hair, the green eyes— dancing, it seemed to him, in the brilliant sunlight as she spotted him and immediately came over. He nodded hello.

"Mr. Adams, what a nice surprise! Actually, I'd been hoping I might see you again."

"I'm still here, miss."

"Kelly O'Shay. Fie on you, sir, for forgetting my name!" Her laughter was childlike in its freshness.

"Have you seen the whole carnival?" he asked.

"Pretty much." She had come closer, letting her voice get louder, it seemed to Clint. He wondered if it was because she wanted anyone nearby to see their relationship was quite casual.

In fact, in the next moment, she lowered her voice to a confiding tone, saying, "I need to see you. But away from prying eyes and ears." And then, suddenly laughing, she spoke in her loud voice again: "How have you been, sir?"

Clint followed suit, playing the game right along with her. At the same time that he was admiring her alertness, he was also taking in her good looks, her figure, the very animal atmosphere that she exuded. Much as he had been with Norah Caldwell in his thoughts only a moment before, the sudden presence of the red-headed

Kelly O'Shay took over, and he felt his passion rising without any instruction whatsoever from his thought, will, or intention.

"Let's find a place where we can talk," he said. "Maybe back in town. I could meet you at that cafe across from the hotel."

"In a half-hour?"

"See you there." Touching the brim of his Stetson, he left her and wandered over to have a look at the "Asiatic Tiger: Captured in the African Jungle after Killing Three Men and Maiming Two Others!" Or so the sign read.

At that point a voice behind him said, "Clint Adams?" And he turned to face a man he had seen two or three times in the crowd and had wondered slightly if he'd been keeping an eye on him. It was evident now that his hunch had been correct.

"What is it?" Clint asked, in a not overly friendly tone. "You had to work up your courage to finally talk to me?"

The man was short and thin, with a scraggly beard and a vague smile in his eyes and at the corners of his mouth; but Clint could see clearly that there was no smile in his self.

"I saw you were busy, mister. So I waited."

"What do you want?"

"The Reverend would like to see you, Adams. I was sent to give you the message."

"So why doesn't the Reverend come and speak to me like you? Is he also afraid?"

Clint watched the little eyes of the other man tighten as he said, "The Reverend is in that wagon down at the end there; the one with the red lines on the spokes."

Clint turned and started away.

"Adams!"

Then, suddenly, another voice cut in: "That will be enough, Burl. Leave it!"

Clint had turned back now and found himself facing a lean gentleman with a big jaw and big ears lying close to his tall head, which was thatched with gray hair, duplicated in his strenuous goatee, which was now bobbing as its owner chewed rapidly, as though trying to remove something that had been caught in his teeth.

"Mr. Adams, I am the Reverend Crispus Quinn. I apologize for the unseemly manners of this, uh, servant of the Lord, but the error in his approach was due to zeal rather than animosity, let me assure you. May I have a word with you?"

"Shoot."

"I feel that you are on your way somewhere and I might be delaying you."

"That is correct." Clint's tone was neutral—neither friendly nor hostile—as he surveyed the strange figure of the Reverend and the somewhat dashed figure of the messenger named Burl.

"I had hoped we could sit down and have a talk. I've an interesting proposition to make to you. Could you spare me just ten, fifteen minutes of your valuable time?"

The voice that came from the hard, thin lips was soft with insistence and the suggestion of mysterious importance.

Clint was tempted to say no, just in order to establish the situation on his terms. But the Gunsmith was anything but a pigheaded man, and he saw the sense in bending a little. He nodded. "I have about ten minutes."

The thin lips smiled as the Reverend stepped smartly back and gave a small bow of appreciation. Then, his hands clasped together in front of him, he led the way to the wagon with the red stripes on its spokes.

It was warm inside the Reverend's wagon. There were carpets and two holy pictures on a small stand. The Reverend Quinn lighted a candle as he entered, for the interior was otherwise gloomy, with the canvas down over the entrance. There was the smell of some kind of incense.

Clint accepted the low stool offered by his host, who sat on another stool on which were two cushions.

"Would you join me in a libation?" The voice was sonorous.

"I only have a few minutes, remember?" Clint said pleasantly. "So I reckon not. Let's get to what you've got on your mind."

The Reverend's big teeth flashed at that, as though he appreciated the Gunsmith's remark—sticking to his guns, as it were.

"I wanted to talk to you about the possibility of hiring on with the caravan, at least while we're here in Little Horn."

"Doing what?" Clint asked, as if he didn't very well know.

"Doing guns. I have heard of you, sir. I have heard that you are sometimes called the Gunsmith, meaning, I presume, that you not only are a dead shot but could also possibly give lessons to others who would wish to improve their pistol abilities. Is this not so, sir?"

"Not so," the Gunsmith said, shaking his head.

"The emolument would not be small, I assure you, for there would be—provided, of course, that you agree—there would be the lessons that I would wish to take myself."

At this the Gunsmith took pause, for he could hear the tone of something else in what the Reverend was saying. Obviously there was something more than merely what had been said. Something was very much implied; and because it was ambiguous, it was all the more on target. The warning rang through Clint Adams like a gong.

"I'll turn it over," he said. "What I can teach is how to repair a weapon. The maintenance is—as likely you know—the basic importance with guns. You've got a poor weapon, you don't have a chance."

"Yes, I understand that you also do gun repair, rebuilding, and all that. And that too could be part of our arrangement— should we come to that," he added quickly.

"One thing I am making clear," Clint said. "My gun is not for hire."

"But there was no suggestion of that, sir!" The alarm in the Reverend's voice took over the atmosphere.

Clint had risen and, with a nod at the still seated Reverend, he started toward the double door at the front of the wagon.

"Sir, will you at least think about it? I feel certain that we can work something out. You see, there is such a need for *intelligent* instruction in respect to firearms. Do you catch my drift, Adams? Sir! The *misuse* of firearms is the great blight on our civilization. Sir, it is in the service of control, of judicious management of oneself and one's weapons, that I, as a man of God, am trying to bring the message to the wilderness. The message 'Thou Shalt Not Kill'! I need your help, sir. The Lord needs your help, Mr. Adams. I beg you not to turn your back on my request but to give me another hearing when you have more time."

He stood there in front of Clint, his hands clasped together in front of him, his eyes, his whole body, beseeching.

"I'll turn it over," Clint said again. Then, ducking his head slightly to avoid a lamp bracket, he stepped out into the daylight.

"Thank you, thank you, sir!" The words followed after him like someone calling.

Clint realized he'd have to hurry not to keep Kelly O'Shay waiting. He had a strong feeling that she had something important to say to him.

FIVE

Clint had decided on the O.K. Cafe in which to meet Kelly. It was the place where he'd had coffee with Norah, from which they'd left abruptly when he'd had the feeling that there was something fishy going on. When the thought of going there had first flashed into his mind, he'd told himself it would be better not to. But then a second thought had supplanted that one: Why not? Was there some connection with the cafe—and its strange owner—and some of the people in town who were obviously concerned by the presence of the Gunsmith? Why not try a little flushing of the bird?

She was waiting for him, seated at a table talking to the plump girl who had dissolved in giggles as the proprietor had tried bullying her the last time Clint was there.

"I want you to meet my friend Felice," Kelly said. "This is Clint Adams."

Felice beamed at him. Though pudgy, she had—like

61

many fat people—a special grace about her. She seemed to move effortlessly as she disappeared into the kitchen to get their order.

Instantly, an uproar ensued, and they heard the voice of Emile, weeping and wailing that the girl didn't do enough and left everything to him.

"Just like last time I was here," Clint said with a grin.

Kelly lifted her eyebrows just a little. "So you know them? The famous happily married couple."

"They're married?"

"Happily. Believe it or not."

There was a sudden silence from the kitchen, and then they heard a great smack, like a paddle landing on a side of beef. Then silence.

"I'd better take a look," Clint said, getting quickly to his feet. "He might really have hurt her."

"I doubt it," Kelly said calmly.

And she was proven right. To the Gunsmith's astonishment, it was Emile who was holding his side and leaning weakly against the table, while Felice was coolly washing her hands in the tub of water on the range.

"A little love pat," she explained sweetly as she saw the astounded expression on the face of Clint Adams.

"Love pat, indeed!" roared Emile in pain and outrage. "She hit me with that paddle!" He was still holding his side, still leaning on the table. "I will beat you tonight, my love!"

"Hah!" Drying her hands, she crossed the room and poured from the pot of coffee, then handed him a mug. "Drink this, my love, while I attend to our customers."

"Ah yes . . ." Smiling, he touched the side of her shoulder with his pudgy fingers, then regarded her mobile buttocks as she picked up two coffee mugs for the customers and walked into the other room.

"Life, my friend," he said, with a wry smile at the Gunsmith, "is full of surprises. Especially for one who marries a woman thirty years younger."

"I'll have to take your word for that, Emile," Clint said soberly.

Emile smiled as the girl walked back into the kitchen. "Your coffee is served, sir," she said, with a smile for Clint.

Emile was now beaming. "Ah, my love. In Italy, I assure you, things are different."

"You're not in Italy now, Emile my dear."

Then, all at once, he had changed, just as Clint started to the door and turned, pausing in the doorway.

Emile had walked forward and, reaching up, stroked his hand alongside his wife's head. "Cara mia."

And suddenly she was in his arms, weeping.

Clint Adams left them.

"There's something wrong with her, isn't there?" he asked Kelly when he sat down.

"She is crazy, but not all the time. She has fits."

"But one can see he loves her."

"They love each other."

He nodded, and his gaze was vague for a moment, as though he were trying to remember something.

"What is it?" she asked.

"I think I've got it. Last time I was in here, I heard a strange noise out in the kitchen and thought that there was a third person there. But it could have been her."

"She could have been having one of her attacks," the girl said.

"Do you know them well?"

"I know Felice. You see, she's a little bit like my sister, whom I mentioned to you—Millie. Millie isn't well, either. She's deaf, and she has trouble speaking. It's why I need money. And maybe it's also why I sympathize with Emile and Felice. I don't know."

They were silent for another moment or so, and then he asked, "What did you want to see me about?"

Leaning forward a little, she said in a low voice, "I have to tell you that my, uh, employer has told me to see you again."

"I knew you wouldn't be able to make a break for it."

"Like I told you, I need—"

"The money. I know."

"I can't stay long. He wants to set me up with you and let him know everything you say and do. Hell, I don't know what he really wants."

He watched the tears swell in her eyes, and he looked away. "Who is it?" he asked, his eyes swinging back to her.

"I don't know. He sends somebody."

"But how did they pick on you? Why you?"

"It was after I went down to Louise's and asked for work."

"Louise's?"

"She runs one of the cathouses. There are two in town. Plus some individuals."

"But why didn't you set up on your own? Why go to work for someone you have to give a cut to?"

"You have to, it seems, if you don't know the ropes. If you're green. As I obviously am to them."

"What did Louise tell you then?"

"She listened to what I had to say and then told me to wait till I heard from her."

"And . . . ?"

"The next thing was a visit from a man whose name I didn't catch, or maybe he didn't even give it. I don't remember. He said he came from Louise and then he told me to meet you, and the rest you know."

"You've seen the same man since? Was it the same one who told you to look me up again?"

She nodded.

"And now what? You'll tell him you met with me?"

"I'll have to. I just wish I . . ." She paused, and he finished for her.

"You wish you'd decided on a different career."

"I guess that's the best way to put it," she said wryly.

"You've no notion who is behind the man and Louise?"

"I don't even know if there is someone behind, as you put it."

"Well, we'd better part company for the moment, my friend," he said. "I've got some things to attend to. And also I've got to do a good bit of thinking. Somebody seems very interested in my being here in Little Horn."

"I'd say that, if you asked me," she said with a wry smile. "I wish I could help you somehow."

"I wish I could help you, too."

She lifted her hands, the smile still on her face, and gave a little shrug. Then they both laughed.

"Look," Clint said, "let's make a pact. All right?"

"I like you." She had leaned forward on her forearms and was looking directly into his eyes.

"Same here. I like you too." He grinned at her. "But now look. We've got to use our heads. You've got to have something to tell this man, whatever his name is, who told you to watch me."

"And get to know you."

"Right. Now, what will you tell him?"

"That you're especially good-looking, sir."

"I'm serious."

"So am I."

He looked at her then directly, his eyes feeling her face. "And so are you. But we have to be sensible," he said, reaching for his cup of coffee. "I know what you could tell him. Tell him I said I was going out of town for a day or two."

"Are you? I mean, really?"

He nodded. "I am going out of town. I don't know for how long, is all."

"Will I see you when you get back?"

"That's your job, isn't it?"

"That's my pleasure, Mr. Adams."

They both grinned at that.

"See if you can catch anything on who your friend is working for."

"I'll surely try. Do you have anyone special in mind?"

"I don't know anybody in town, really, but I'd guess somebody important. Somebody sees me as being in the way of something, I don't know what. Anyway, keep your ears open. And mostly, take care of yourself. Got it?"

"I do."

"Now, you leave and I'll stay a bit, then head for my room at the Drovers'. They'll figure maybe you'll be coming there."

"Is that what you want me to do?" she asked simply.

"I won't be there," he said. "But we want to keep the game going."

"I see."

"You go there, and maybe the room clerk will tell you I'm not in. Maybe he won't. You'll see. But you play it as though you were planning to see me and I was expecting you." He held up his finger. "What I am saying is, you play it that way. Don't go into my room. If the room clerk lets you upstairs, then knock on the door, but do not go in."

"Why?"

He had the feeling that he had frightened her a little. "First of all, I won't be there. But somebody else might be. I don't know. I don't know who these people are or what they're liable to do. See? And I want you to cover yourself. And not get hurt."

"I'll be all right."

"Make sure. I'm not trying to frighten you, but make very sure."

"I will."

After she was gone, he ordered another cup of coffee. It was time to get out of town, he told himself. Time to go visit Chance Casper and get a few things straightened out: about Knox's outfit, about the three 88 yahoos who tried to set him up for either a beating or a bushwhacking. And maybe Kelly would gain him a little time.

He stood up just as Felice, the waitress, came back into the front room.

"Not a good time for business, I reckon, with most folks over to the carnival," he said.

"It's all right with me," she replied. "I'm overworked, and I can use an easy day, sir."

Clint grinned at her.

"You happen to know a man named Chance Casper?" he asked, figuring full well that she had to but wanting to open something.

"I do," she said. "There is three of his handy men just crossed the street, heading this direction. You can use the back door if you want. I can tell 'em you went back to the outhouse."

As he swept past her, the Gunsmith reached out and touched her arm. Emile already had the back door open for him, and he closed it swiftly as Clint passed through.

"What I am saying is that he is one slippery one, that one." It was Burt Clancy speaking, standing swing-hipped in front of Chance Casper, who was listening.

They were in one of the corrals at the 88 slash, surrounded by Chance Casper country, Chance Casper livestock, Chance Casper cowhands, outriders, gunmen, and whatever else was necessary to keep one of the biggest outfits in western Wyoming going.

Casper was thinking just that as he listened to the words that came stiffly from the tight lips of his foreman. And he was thinking, too, how it wasn't really so. Not any more. Not with his note at the bank sticking into him like a goddamn gun barrel. By

God into his eye, his ear, up his ass! He was covered! Hell, he couldn't even scratch!

He said nothing of this to Clancy. He wouldn't even have said anything to God. Tough, he was. One of the oldtimers; and by God he'd even it, somehow! Somehow!

"And what about those boys you sent over to the Hollinger spread? What are they doing now? I ain't heard a thing from Adams."

"Me neither," Clancy said, trying to see how he could slide off the subject of how the three had messed up the confrontation with Clint Adams. "But the boys did deliver your message."

"Fat lotta good it did. Who were those knotheads?"

"Jake, Chuck, and Lolly."

"Jesus! And three of them couldn't handle it. Clancy, this here's turnin' into a dead hoss and a whip, and I ain't about to take and whip the shit out of all of yez to get some action going here!"

Clancy had already prepared himself for the outburst he'd been expecting. Still, he wasn't happy. "Some of them I do admit, is piss-poor, Mr. Casper. But they be what's about. A good hand is hard to find. I mean, a man who can throw a rope, bust a hoss, ride the line, and handle a weapon—he is rare." And then, not liking that he chose to say it, he added, "They don't make 'em like that any more."

"That I do know," his employer said, pleased but careful. He cut his gaze swiftly to his foreman to check on his sincerity. Burt Clancy's face was as open and sincere as a sober preacher's.

But Clancy had to work at it. It was sure no Fourth of

July working for a man like Chance Casper, especially
with him having the goddamn bank jumping up his
ass. Clancy, who always had difficulty in hiding his
true feelings—and he knew it all too well—made
himself think of his mother. For he knew that damn
Casper could pick a thought right out of a man's head,
he was that sharp.

It was just at that moment that the foreman saw relief
was at hand.

"Rider coming," he said, glancing off to Casper's
left. But he had let his feeling of relief come in
too soon.

"Wondered when you were going to notice it," Casper
said, cold as a block of ice. "They signaled from the
butte a good two, three minutes ago."

With his eyes hard as bullets and his face tight as the
stretched hide on a pannier, he gave one look at his
foreman, turned, and walked toward his ranch house.

"Not just the town, my dear, not just the town, but
very much of the basin, too."

Tennessee Fitz's thick palm patted the firm but not
hard buttocks of the young woman standing in her
chemise beside his easy chair.

She was tall, regal—after all, her billing said she
was a "countess"—and her figure exemplified all that
could ruin the morality of any man.

"Of course, darling, I have heard in many places of
how you have brought great things to the frontier."

"Great things?" He beamed at her, wanting more.

"Plans. Care for the people who come. Making peace
with the savages and all that. And developing this

wilderness into a civilized country. All that. It is a proud thing!" Her accent was tinted just enough to cause the listener to raise his attention.

His eager eyes fell on her nipples, thrusting against the silk chemise, and he felt his excitement accelerating. But Tennessee Fitz also had business in mind, and while his sexual appetite began to stir again, he cautioned himself not to be foolish but to get his plan moving first. The Countess Maritza was definitely part of his plan.

He moved back in his chair a little, watching her as she drew on her cigar. "Of course, my dear, as I have told you, I will help you in any way I can. You have my word on it."

"I know. I trust you completely, Feetz, dear!"

"Let me see that paper again." He half turned toward the table at his side, where her reticule lay with the paper she had shown him, giving her title to the acreage in question.

"Here." She swiftly plucked the document out of her bag and handed it to him. Drawing up a chair, she sat down opposite, leaning forward with her forearms on her knees, her superb cleavage within inches of his appreciative eyes.

Tennessee Fitz forced his eyes away from the delight of her creamy bust and onto the equally delightful prospect of the great wealth that, according to his most reliable reports, lay beneath the land left the lady by her late husband.

"You have told me everything?" He raised his eyes to look into hers, searching for honesty—or at any rate, sincerity.

"I have told you everything I know. It is the

place Serge, my husband, discovered when he was
hunting out here in the West with Mr.—who did I
say?—ah yes, Hickok! Mr. Wild Hickok."

"Wild Bill."

"Wild Beel! That is the one. And he found this land.
He—how you say?—laid it."

"Laid claim to it," Fitz corrected.

"But not Wild Beel—it was Serge, my husband,
discovered! Darling Feetz!" And she swept his fingers
to her lips, then rubbed his hand along her cheek. "I
know you would help me!"

Tennessee found he was having trouble keeping his
mind on business. At the same time, he had a question
that he could not settle.

"Tell me why you don't just sell the land. I mean,
you live in France. What good can it do you here?"

"Ah, it is just as I tell you. My advisor, Boris—I
told you of him. He suggest, 'Maurie, why not have a
nice pied-à-terre here in the Wild West, where you can
vacation from time to time.' And I agree." Her dark,
liquid eyes covered his face. "And of course, darling,
where I meet this wonderful man, Feetz, who helps me
and now who I can visit with him in my pied-à-terre!
Beautiful, non?"

"It is beautiful," Tennessee was saying, almost
lapping her words, as his eyes played on her bosom. "It
is fortunate, my dear Maritza—Maurie—that we
have met. I can help you. And, uh, you can help me."

"How? How can I help you, wonderful mans!"

His hand slipped along her thigh as he edged closer.

"Ach, but of course! It will be my pleasure, too!"

But once again, Fitz was reminded of business, so he

said, "There is a man I want you to contact." When she looked puzzled, he said, "*Find*. Find him and get to know him."

She had slipped forward in her seat, so that his hand was now able to move farther up her thigh. "But of course, my friend, my dear, my Tenny-see! Tell me what you wish."

"I'll go into that later," said Tennessee Fitz, as her hand moved along his thigh and grasped his erection, which was bulging in his pants.

Surely, he decided, he had given enough time and thought and attention to business—for the moment. And anyway, whether he had or not was of small moment now, as he rose and brought her to her feet. Without any further conversation, they moved into another room, undressing as they went.

"On the bear," she said. "I want you on the bear!"

He was only too happy to oblige, as she lay down on her back on the bearskin, opening her legs. Then suddenly, she took his member and guided it to her mouth, accepting it greedily. Her tongue fluttering along his shaft, he stroked in and out, his senses pounding wildly all through his body and all but bringing him to a climax.

But she was an expert at timing, and withdrawing her mouth, she turned so that he could plunge his face into her bush. Which he did eagerly. And the two of them sucked each other into oblivion, their bodies afire with the great streaming delight that ran through each of them and into the other.

For several moments they lay together, spent in their ecstasy.

Returned to sanity, Tennessee Fitz was already thinking of his next moves.

"This man I want you to watch," he began.

"Darling, I will do anything you want. Only, could we not wait more moments before business?"

Her hand was already stroking him, and he was already erect—surprised at himself, in fact. It had been a long time since he'd managed such frequency in such a short space of time. Still, it had been a long time since he'd seen a body like the one that was now offering itself for entry on its hands and knees. So there was nothing to do but mount her—from the rear, as requested—and to hell with business. It could wait. He had it all set up. It was all set . . . it was ready . . . he was ready . . . and he could 'tend to it later . . . later . . . and deeper . . . and faster . . . and O God, what delicious delight . . . delishdelite . . . light . . . and more and more and more . . . and to hell with business . . . I didn't mean that . . . to hell I didn't . . . yes, yes, yes . . . and to hell with the damn gold . . . I didn't mean that . . . didn't . . . did . . . did, did, did . . . the gold . . . old . . . old gold . . . and oh . . . oh . . . oh . . .

The mountainman, the trapper, the gold seeker, the buff hunter, and finally the cattleman. Chance Casper. Originally from the Red River country. Born and growed a "Texian." And never had he been any otherwise, as it was said.

He had trailherded north with his dad, now dead and a good piece of the folklore; he'd fought the Comanche, the Kiowa, the Cheyenne, and the Sioux. Trailherding had been his education, bred into the blood. But from the moment he'd seen the Stinking Water country he had known it was here he'd throw his brand.

The Indians, the outlaws, the other cattlemen had not seen it that way, but it had not deterred Chance Casper. He had fought . . . and won. But the West was changing, and he, Casper, was challenged. Challenged in a way that it was difficult for him to handle. Chance was a shrewd man, but he was never subtle. He could handle the red man, the outlaw, and even the lawman; but the homesteader, the farmer, the sodbuster, and that vague resource of every damn thief who's made his way west—the Law—was something new and, to use his own word, "angrifying."

He had found a way around. Stake a forty-and-found cowpoke and he'd work up a section of land and sell it back to you. That way nobody could accuse you of land-grabbing. In fact, you even got credit for giving a young cow waddie a helping hand. Except that sonofabitch Caldwell had struck out on his own, selling off a piece to that other bastard, the new marshal, Hollinger. Fact, he'd even wondered if it hadn't been Hollinger who'd put Caldwell up to it. And so his plan for controlling the whole of the basin had gone bust. Well, he would try again. Only now, with the bank jumping up his ass, he was up the creek for damn sure. Unless he could figure something. Because, by God, a man who'd built something had to keep going. And he would. He was!

Chance Casper sat in his office in the big log ranch house, staring into his rolltop desk. He didn't need that desk; he did all his business in his head. But Emily had gotten it for him at some auction, saying he ought to have it. But he was no bookkeeping man. A long way from that! The saddle, not the chair, was his place. Except that he was older now, and he couldn't handle things the way he had in the old days. He knew that too well. And he was not at all happy about the older years seeping in like that. First thing you know, hell, it'd be all over. And he still had work to do.

He sat there, a tall, leather-lean man, honed by the years on the trail, the dust of horses and cows, the stink of men under fire—not only the fire of guns, but liquor and not enough grub to go round—and only the hard ground for resting and tobacco juice rubbed into the eyes to stay awake against stampedes, Indians, outlaws, electrical storms, flash floods, heat, hunger, and whatever else Fate had to throw at you. A man with a boney face, deep-socketed eyes, a longhorn mustache, and knobby hands with big veins. He sat there in the old swivel chair—which had come with Emily's desk—chewing on an unlit cigar, as he generally did whenever he had what he called "studying" to put on a situation.

He let his dark eyes wander to the open window now. It was just getting to be dawn, and he could smell the fresh-cut hay that had been rained on slightly during the night; it would need to be turned before the sun burned it.

A step outside on the porch, followed by a knock.

"Come," he called out.

It was Burt Clancy who entered.

Casper swung around in his chair to face his foreman. "Well?"

Clancy was shaking his head, looking down at the floor as though in search of an explanation. "They bungled it again."

"God dammit!"

"They were right on top of him. He was having coffee with O'Shay. Then she left, and the boys closed in. I told them to bring him out here if they had to hog-tie him."

"And he got away."

Chance Casper stood in front of his foreman, hard as a gun barrel. Indeed, Clancy might have preferred facing a loaded shotgun rather than Mr. Casper at that particular moment.

His employer did not say anything. He simply struck a wooden lucifer and lit his cigar. He blew out two or three rings of blue smoke and then took the cigar out of his mouth. His eyes were still on Burt Clancy.

"Jesus Henry Christ!" he said. His face etched in disgust, he turned back to the window, where he stood staring out as his foreman closed the door behind him.

Chance Casper continued to stand there at the window as the rider on the big black horse disappeared from view behind a stand of box elders. Casper saw that he was going to follow the road around the north side of the ranch houses.

And now, even though the rider was out of sight, Chance Casper continued to stay at the window, while the Gunsmith rode closer.

SIX

It hadn't been difficult shaking the three. He had watched them from the tableland north of town as they tried cutting his trail. He'd confused them easily. The creek had helped, as had the false trail he'd left outside the livery: He'd dropped a package of his makings, as though he'd been in a big hurry, leaving prints in the soft area just outside the corral in back of the barn; then he'd cut clear on firm terrain around the back of the town and ridden through the creek for some time.

Now, riding up from a different creek, past the big butte and out in full view of the 88 Slash, he knew he was being watched. But it was the time for boldness, and he was counting on Casper's curiosity. The man evidently needed him somehow, or he wouldn't have sent the invitation.

Now the sun was up and it was warm on his back. When he leaned forward, bending his head, he felt it on the back of his neck. His eye caught a rider off to his left just slipping down a draw, while to his right another sat his horse, motionless.

When he reached the box elders and dropped below sight of the ranch houses, he felt more at ease, although he knew that of course he was still being watched. He hurried Duke's gait a little and rode up a shallow draw to come suddenly right upon the corral, the barn, and then what appeared to be the 88's bunkhouse. It'd been unexpected, and he smiled to himself. After all, it was the unexpected that a man had to expect.

And suddenly there they were: half a dozen men coming out of the bunkhouse to stand there facing him, their hands close to their gunbelts.

The Gunsmith didn't hesitate. He rode right up to those men and drew rein.

"I have come to see Chance Casper," he said.

A man stepped forward. "You can tell me your business, mister. I be the foreman here."

"I said I want to see Casper," the Gunsmith said.

"I'll tell you again, mister. My name is Clancy, foreman for Mr. Casper. He is busy now."

Clint surveyed the group of six men, taking each one in turn—checking their facial expression, the stance, the placement of their handguns.

"Drop yer gun, Gunsmith, and I might take a look-see if Mr. Casper is around."

Suddenly one of the other men spoke. "There is six of us, Gunsmith. You can't get us all!"

"Arnold, shut yer mouth!" snapped Clancy.

But he had taken his attention away from the Gunsmith, who in that instant had drawn his six-gun to cover the foreman of the 88. A shock seemed to rush through the entire group. Clancy paled as he saw the gun pointed at him.

"Mr. Clancy, I make it a rule not to draw my gun without shooting it. You want to disappoint me, don't you?"

He watched the foreman's Adam's apple pump a couple of times. "Unbuckle. All of you, or you'll be needing a new foreman."

As they did so, out of the side of his eye, Clint saw the door of the big house open and a man appear.

"Clancy, God dammit, what'n hell's name do you think yer doin'!"

Clancy and his men had already dropped their gun-belts. Clint Adams, swiftly holstering his gun, stepped down from his horse.

Chance Casper's angry stride had carried him right into the center of the action, and he now faced his foreman, his face red and his jaw working as he seemed to be getting his angry words ready for another barrage.

But he didn't say anything further to Clancy or the men. Instead, he turned to Clint Adams and said, "I apologize for my men's behavior, sir. Mr. Adams, is it, I do believe?"

But the Gunsmith did not pick up on the hospitality. "Casper, I want to know what your men were doing over at the R Bar O."

The rancher was clearly taken aback by the sudden confrontation, though he held his ground. "I sent them with an invite, like I reckon they told you."

Clint had kept his attention on Clancy and his men, not leaving them for a second, and now as one man at the far end made a movement, he snapped out, "You stand still!" Then, turning back to Casper, he said, "I prefer to talk with you privately."

"Good! We'll go inside."

Clint had ground-hitched Duke, and now he picked up his reins and led him to a hitching rack outside the big house, where he loosened his cinch, then tightened it again. He knew his horse would be ready.

The men had still not moved, though Clancy, plenty put out by the way the Gunsmith had taken over, was impatient.

"I see you're a man of the old school," Casper said as he led the way into the house and then down the short hall and into his office.

"Do you mean the school of hard knocks?" Clint said, amused by the change in Casper.

The cattleman nodded to a chair and sat himself at his desk. He opened a drawer, from which he brought forth a bottle and two glasses. "I mean the school where men were men and the women liked 'em that way," he said, pouring in accompanient to the old saying.

"The old days," repeated Clint, with a rueful smile and a sigh. "I believe in right here and now."

"So do I," said Casper firmly, moving to a chair opposite his visitor after handing him his drink. "I admire the way you handled those men, Adams." He looked down at his glass, which he was holding in both hands. "I'd like to drink a toast."

"To what?"

Chance Casper lifted his glass of whiskey. His eyes went to the big window, which was filled with the deep blue sky and the far mountains. "The country is changing, Adams. You know that same as me."

"I do."

The cattleman lifted his glass. "To the wonderful country. To the way it is now, and the way it was then."

And for that very short moment, Clint Adams saw a different Chance Casper. Yet he didn't make the mistake of thinking that the man who gave the toast was the man with whom he would be dealing.

Suddenly he felt a cat brush against his leg, purring softly.

"You got a way with animals, Adams. I'll bet you wouldn't want to sell that black horse of yours."

"No more than I'd sell my gun, Casper."

The whiskey was good quality, and it was circulating nicely through him, as he watched the cattleman working up to what he wanted to say.

"That's good whiskey, Casper."

"The best, in my view."

"Mind if I give a toast now?" Clint asked.

"Why, go right ahead." To Clint's surprise, there was a trace of a smile in the other man's face. He hadn't expected that after the remark he'd made about not selling his gun.

"I liked your toast," Clint said. "I'd just like to add something to it." He raised his glass, and Casper followed suit. He saw the brindle cat jump up onto the windowsill, stretch, and start washing a paw.

"To the wonderful country—yes, for sure. And to the people from whom we stole it."

He watched the cattleman's glass freeze in midair.

"I ain't drinking to the health of no goddamn Injuns, by God!"

"Don't." Clint was smiling as he drank.

"What kind of crazy talk is that, for Christ sake! Goddamn thieving, murdering sonsofbitches! And you expect me to drink a toast to them! You're crazy!"

Clint stood up, looking across at his host. "No, Casper. It's you who is crazy."

"Me!"

"You want me working with you. You want to hire me. You claim I'm crazy. But if I'm crazy, then only a crazy man would hire me. You get me!" Those three last words drilled right across the room.

The cattleman looked as though he'd been struck dumb. Clint had the impulse to laugh, though not from thinking anything was funny. He said, "I don't care who you drink to or don't drink to. But I think I've shown you where you stand with me." His eye was suddenly caught by the picture of the woman on top of the rolltop desk. He felt Casper's eyes on him, and when he turned away from the photograph, he saw that the rancher was indeed looking directly at him.

Chance Casper's voice had a tired sound to it when he spoke. "I don't hold with them red devils. The land is here, and we took it—yes, on account of we were tougher and smarter, and anyways we won it. Now it's ourn'. It's still the wonderful country, and nobody's gonna give it back." He looked down at his drink, then looked up at the Gunsmith, who was still standing. His voice was different now, as he said, "I need you, Adams. I do. And it ain't the Injuns that's the trouble."

"You sound like you want me real bad."

"I reckon I do."

"I told you my gun is not for hire."

"That's what I know."

"And you still want me anyway."

"I do."

Clint caught Casper's streaking glance in the direction of the photograph.

"Will you join me in a toast?"

"Not like that one."

It was the answer that Clint had expected.

"Then I'll have to offer a different toast." The Gunsmith raised his glass. "To the wonderful country. And to whatever or whoever it was that made it wonderful and will keep it."

He watched Casper nod and then lift his glass and drink from it. His breath came out in a little gasp as he put his glass down.

Funny, Clint was thinking, how a man could agree with something without even suspecting it.

"So tell me what you want, Casper."

The big sign on the side of the Conestoga read: "THE GAMBLER'S DEN OF INIQUITY! An educational institution guaranteed to help the gambling addict to defeat his destructive habit and to cleanse his soul of the curse that will inevitably lead him to the devil's pit! Based on the same principles as the famously successful Keeley Cure for smoking."

Inside the opening to the wagon a second sign, prominently displayed, offered the stark statement in large, bold letters: "CAVEAT EMPTOR!" Underneath, the translation into English—"Let the Buyer Beware"— made certain that the imposing Latin declaration was not lost upon the uneducated. Surely, it added quality—if not a hint of fear, of excitement—to the premises.

Indeed, from time to time, when asked why he should be including a gambling establishment in his entourage, the Reverend Crispus Quinn would point out that the gambling addict who ventured within the premises would learn a lesson he would never forget; and he would never gamble again.

This admonishment against the gambling habit, when delivered to the curious—who occasionally happened to be wearing the tokens of the law—by the tall man of saintly appearance, gentle voice, and benevolent mien, generally turned the questioner away, often apologizing for having misunderstood the high purpose of the proposed endeavor that was being delivered by this imposing man of the cloth.

At present, within the Den a group of earnest poker players sat hunched around a baize-top table while a few hangers-on watched the proceedings.

The game was jacks or better, and the action of the moment, which was brisk, included those three whiskey-haulers: Stinking Water Josh Hissinger, Honey Mellody, and Grizzly Poland.

Having delivered their valuable cargo into expectant hands—that is, to those who would turn the whiskey into money across the counter—the three were enjoying the fruits of their efforts. Of course, first of all, they had handed all the money over to the Reverend Quinn, who then dispensed their pay so that they could spend it in the Gambler's Den of Iniquity; and perhaps thus learn a valuable lesson.

The boys didn't care about such niceties; they were enjoying themselves. And as Stinking Water Josh, a natural born philosopher, had pointed out often enough, "Money is made to be spent, and life is meant to be fun. God dammit!"

Grizzly and Honey agreed wholly with this sage dictum from their elder, who had learned it as a button way up north on the Stinking Water River—hence his moniker—from his grandfather, who had also included the injunction that "it don't hurt to know everything."

Stinking Water's two sidekicks believed completely in these sage observations. And tomorrow, being Sunday, they would all listen to the Reverend deliver a bang-up sermon on the evils of drink, gambling, fornicating, and a number of other, perhaps lesser though still compelling, pleasures.

At the moment, however, they were addressing themselves to the task of "teaching" a brace of would-be gamblers the lesson so boldly advertised on the poster outside. That is to say, they were not only enjoying themselves but were stripping the two "unfortunates" pretty much down to the bone.

It was Stinking Water's deal. Accepting the cards, he raised his impressive eyebrows and grinned. He had two front teeth missing, and one eye drooped—a great face for frightening young children. Adroitly, his leathery hands shuffled, cut, dealt. Then he sat back, lowering his shoulders to let his companions know—in case they might have missed it—that he had buried the fourth ace, Honey Mellody now having been dealt two, and Stinking Water himself one.

The hand proceeded as planned, and Honey Mellody pulled in the pot. In a little while, the "pupils"—as the

Reverend always referred to the "marks"—succumbed to the poverty of their cards and the game was over.

Later, after the crowd had gone home and night had fallen, the Reverend listened to the report brought by Stinking Water Josh and his two companions.

"I take it that you were scrupulous in following your instructions," he said.

"Screw . . . ?" Stinking Water's jaw fell open as his mind raced, trying to put together some kind of meaning for the jawbreaker that the Reverend had used.

"I mean, you paid close attention to my instructions," the Reverend said, his words falling harshly inside the wagon. "That you did *not* sell any whiskey to anyone other than the party who usually handles these things."

"Chad Miller," said Honey Mellody. "Like always."

His two companions nodded.

"And that Chad Miller understood that none of this was to be sold or given to Running Lance's tribe."

"Sure," mumbled Stinking Water.

The Reverend shot a cold eye at the acknowledged leader of the three. "I hope it was and that it still is quite clear that no whiskey must be sold or given to the Indians!"

Those words, resonating within the stuffy Conestoga wagon, carried the full weight of Crispus Quinn's calling. "Otherwise, we will have the army and who knows who else after us in spades. You men understand me?"

"We do," the three answered in perfect unison. After all, they had gone through this exercise a number of times already. And not only with the Reverend, but with others who had hired their wagon and team of mules: their whiskey train, as it was known throughout that part of the country. The three were well known for their ability to haul large amounts of liquor to designated customers—the army, civilians, the railroad teams laying track—but always under the strict admonishment that not a drop must pass to the tribes. The three followed instructions to the letter. To the letter, but no further, the Reverend had been swift to explain when he'd first encountered them. Because while Stinking Water and his boys were under oath not to allow any whiskey to enter Indian hands, the fact that some of the tribes did seem to acquire it only proved that there was, as the old saying had it, more than one way to skin a cat. After all, what could a man do if his wagon were "attacked" by "Indians," or "outlaws," those middlemen who handled not only the money but the matter of "conscience" if indeed there were any.

"You'll head back to South Pass and pick up another load," the Reverend was saying now as he finished counting the money they had handed him.

"Will you still be here?" asked Grizzly Poland.

"I expect to be. But I expect you to be here, too."

Grizzly looked surprised at this, and he lifted his eyebrows, though without saying a word.

"Your bear, dumb bell," snarled the Reverend.

"Ralph will be all right if I ain't here," Grizzly replied. "I got him real well trained."

"I know that." The Reverend released a sigh. "But —and I have explained this to you before—it is not that I expect your vicious grizzly to run amuck and attack people if you're not about to calm him. It's that the attraction is the fact that you have tamed him. Without you he is nothing. Do you understand? I've explained it so many times!" He glared furiously at Grizzly Poland, who looked as if he hadn't understood a word.

"Hell and damnation! I am going to assume that you understand, dammit! And I shall proceed accordingly!" He stood up, his face even more severe than it already had been. And yet, inside, he was mightily pleased by the amount of money the boys had brought in from this most recent whiskey train.

In another few minutes he had walked down the line of wagons and climbed into the one with the red lines painted along its black spokes. As he entered, ducking his head, a hand reached out from the semidarkness to hand him a glass, from which came the delicious smell of expensive brandy.

The Reverend Crispus Quinn—he had been seriously considering changing his "title" to the *Very* Reverend but was waiting for the best moment—stepped briskly down from the mouth of the Conestoga wagon onto the whiffle tree and then hopped lightly to the ground— lightly for a man of his advanced years, that is. It was dawn, the sun not yet up, but its light was suffusing the already blue sky that seemed to hold the land in a moment that did nothing less than call the attention of every living thing. It did this for the Reverend; it did it for the Black Ace, the Avenging Angel of the Lord. Dressed tightly in his "black gun suit," his white hands, white face, and graying goatee almost stark in comparison, he took in the day, breathing deeply, as though he owned it; or at any rate, as if the moment were for his own unique benefit. He then started toward the area beyond the semicircle of wagons in which he had set up a shooting range for the entertainment and education of the crowd that came to the Great Mystery Carnival—not to forget the profit reaped by the man who had brought both the Lord and such worldly benefits to the West.

As he walked, his stride swinging in time with his brace of holstered sixguns—also black—he thought of Clint Adams, the man known as the Gunsmith. What a coup it would be to get the Gunsmith attached to his entourage! Certainly the countess—Maurie—had thought so!

He had broached the subject with her as they sat drinking the superb sazarac he had brought all the way from Cheyenne. It was his favorite beverage, and he kept himself in good supply. The countess too, was surely a "favorite," even though he was well aware of her need for variety. Yet when she had come to him with her problem of how to recoup the fortune lost when Serge, her husband, had suddenly died overseas and the Russian government had impounded all funds, thus leaving her virtually penniless, the Reverend had sought the advice of the Lord and come up with the suggestion that she join his "Family" in its own unique "opening of the West." The rest had all fallen easily into place.

Now—right now—refreshed after the evening's activities with that superb body, the Reverend, having dropped his nocturnal role as Casanova, returned to the Black Ace. Stepping briskly across the warming prairie, he arrived at the clearing in which the targets had been set up: the bull's-eyes in their black circles drawn on white posters, backed by wooden boards; the bottles on top of railings; the bottles hanging by string or rawhide from the limbs of trees; the playing cards nailed to a fence. The question now was how far he should pace off his shooting distance. Since no one was yet about, he decided to start close up and work backward. Something within him was decidedly against anyone watching him at target practice. It was, of course, why he invariably came this early for his exercise.

And as usual, his foresight proved sensible: His first, second, and third shots were complete misses, not even hitting the widest circle. For his next three, he moved in closer. Although he wore two guns, he was only firing with his right. He had once attempted shooting with his left but stopped when he almost shot his horse, who for some strange reason had decided to crop some of the buffalo grass somewhat near the target.

His next shot hit within the outer circle, while the next lodged closer to the center by about a quarter-inch. Not bad. He decided to leave it at that and now try for one of the bottles. He still had one shot left. But at that moment he heard his horse nicker. Looking over to where the little pinto was grazing, he saw him toss his head and then look back over his shoulder.

"There you are, chéri!"

It was Maritza, dressed to perfection in a riding habit that looked as though it had grown with her fantastic figure. The man in black found himself almost paralyzed with the wonder of his sudden desire—after a night of plenty!—as the countess swept toward him, laughing into the fresh morning air.

"Too bad you weren't here a moment ago, my dear! You would have seen some good shooting."

"But let me see now!"

"It's time for coffee and a chat. I have something I wish to discuss with you."

The countess said nothing to this remark; she simply stood quite still, her eyes moving over the black and white figure standing before her. She was recalling how the night before he had been wearing red, white, and blue apparel while reciting Shakespeare—or possibly somebody like Shakespeare; she wasn't dead sure—in a marvelous voice, while creating the most charming, seductive atmosphere she thought she had ever experienced. Crispus Quinn, the great thespian, had literally swept her off her feet . . . and into bed, where he had indeed performed well. Was that also an act? Did it matter? The satisfaction was tremendous. The Reverend—or whatever the devil he was—was just great.

When they were back inside the wagon, he excused himself and swiftly changed his clothing—back into the simple habit of His Reverence—but not his behavior: As he sat down, his hand lay not so casually on her thigh.

"My dear, I thought you wanted to talk over a cup of coffee," she said whimsically, her breath catching as his hand gave just the suggestion of a stroke. This was no longer the firm hand of the gunfighter in black, or even the soft, pious hand of the cleric, but the warm, searching fingers and palm of an accomplished lover, taking his time, warming the treasure that would shortly be his.

She was surprised when he answered her question, for she'd not expected it. She had hoped for action.

"Maurie . . ."

She said nothing in her disappointment, though she moved away an inch or two.

"You've told me something of your meeting with Tennessee Fitzsimmons—I say, 'something,' " he emphasized dryly, "and that he asked you to keep an eye on Clint Adams."

"The man called Gunmen? You tell me of heem last night. The same?"

"He is indeed. And so what I wish you to do is something very simple."

"I already guess eet: You want me keep eye on both Feetz and the Clintman."

"It's so rewarding to work with you, Maurie. I don't have to explain everything over and over in the finest, most ridiculous detail, as I have to with some. He is the *Gunsmith*, remember. Don't forget your role with each of those. Each one is no fool."

"That I know."

"And neither am I, my dear," the Reverend said firmly.

She grinned up into his face as he drew her to him on the large pile of buffalo rugs. "Then take off that silly clothes you wearing. It gets in the way."

"I thought you liked my costumes," he said playfully. "Last night you liked my Romeo suit, did you not?"

"I like best the suit you were born with, my dear." And she lay back, helping him off with his "holy man suit," as he called it.

The Reverend, the Gunfighter, the Great Thespian loved all his various roles, and he loved money, but perhaps most of all he loved the action, the game of excitement, thrills, and danger. He'd learned it all in the riverboat school where his "father"—if indeed the heavyset Fingers Donohue had been his sire—had taught him from the ground up, since he'd been a button. Crisp had loved every inch, every second, every conquest, and even every loss, though these were few. Quite simply, he loved it all: life, whatever it was that went by that name.

And one of the great criterions was now being afforded him by the delicious, sinuous, highly active yet airily soft body undulating beneath him, as together they found their delightful rhythm. They moved slowly at first, his hands and lips exploring all the places of her fantastic body, while hers teased his testicles, his rump, his stroking stick to the point of delirium.

"There's only one thing I wish," he gasped at her as their bodies pumped in unison.

"What!" she whispered, almost too far gone to even mouth the word.

"I wish I could get more of your teat in my mouth."

"Don't give up."

And when he gave a particularly delicious suck, taking her rigid nipple deeply into his throat, she gasped, "There's something I wish, too!"

"Name it."

"I wish I could get the whole of your cock in my mouth."

"Next time . . . it will have to be next time," he said, hardly able to speak.

She said nothing as she spread her legs beyond any position either of them had yet found available, and he drove his raging member deep, high, and repeatedly into her, coming and coming and coming . . .

• • •

Clint Adams had as good as guessed what Chance Casper was going to say when he'd finally pinned him down to what he actually wanted.

The cattleman didn't take any extra time at all in answering Clint's question.

"I want you to run for town marshal."

"I'd have to be appointed, first of all," Clint said. "And anyway, I don't want the job."

"Shit!" Casper reached for his drink. "You are a pigheaded man, Adams."

"Never mind the compliments, Casper. But I am curious as to why you would want me. Especially since I wouldn't be on your payroll."

"I know you wouldn't be on my payroll, but I know you'd see a fair shake was done. Listen . . ." And he leaned forward, his forearms on his knees. "I ain't a man who generally goes with the law. Never have been. If I had, I wouldn't of never gotten the 88 together, let me tell you. Same time, I don't go for the shit Fitzsimmons tries to pull. And by God, does! Sure, I'd ruther have a man in the marshal's office who was right on my side of the fence, but I can't. So least I can push for is a man who plays it straight!"

"You're telling me you're desperate," Clint said.

A scowl suddenly appeared on the other man's hard face. "Adams, I am asking."

"I know. I know you're not the kind who begs."

A silence fell.

"How come Knox Hollinger got in there?" Clint asked. "I can't see him getting backing from you."

The cattleman studied that for a minute. Then, squinting at Clint, he said, "See, I still got a little pull at Fort McWade. I could recommend you, and I've done the army a couple of turns. You know what I mean."

"I do. They trust you, is what you're saying."

"That's the size of it, I reckon. Anyways, I pushed for Hollinger."

"On account of you wanted his spread."

The rancher nodded.

"Why?"

"It would of rounded off my graze, kept a clear line between two sections of my land. I needed it. Also, I was in debt to the bank, which I am sure you have picked up on by now. I figured I might have a good bargaining position, better'n I had, with Fitzsimmons and the bank if I had Hollinger's place—or at any rate, had Hollinger with me. Plus, like I said, he was a straight-shooter. Trouble was, he was too damn straight."

"How come he got bushwhacked," Clint said, raising his eyebrows.

Casper nodded.

"Who did it?"

"I don't know. Course, right away I suspicioned Fitzsimmons. But I dunno. That ain't enough to go on. I got a notion, though, that some people about figger I had a hand in it."

"Did you?"

The rancher didn't answer. He was looking across the room; Clint thought he might be looking at his rolltop desk.

He waited, and then he felt more than actually saw Chance Casper shake his head very slowly.

"I aim to find out who killed him," Clint said.

"That is what I know."

"I'd appreciate any help you can give me."

After a moment, the rancher said, "He must of owed the bank some, but I doubt they collect in that kind of way. It'd be easy enough to find out."

"Maybe the bank doesn't collect that way, but what about somebody else?"

Chance Casper shrugged, lifting his hands, his eyebrows, and then reached for his drink. "Course, there could be others thinking they might find a use for that land."

"Like, do you mean Fitzsimmons?"

"I don't mean anybody. Exceptin' a man such as Fitzsimmons is one greedy sonofabitch. And I ain't saying anything I wouldn't tell him to his face."

Clint took a pull at his drink and then said, "I understand you're about the oldest party in these parts. Even before Little Horn."

Casper nodded slowly. "I wuz the first one in this country. First white man."

"You come up from Texas with a herd, did you?"

"I sure did. It wasn't no easy thing in those days. These wranglers nowadays, they got no notion what it was to trailherd back then."

Clint took another drink, wanting somehow to get the cattleman to open up.

"When did Fitzsimmons get here?"

"Three, maybe four years back. He started right in grabbing land; promised everybody the railroad was coming, which it didn't. Told everybody Little Horn was going to be a big town, which it never was. Even started talking about maybe there was gold up in Slater's Gulch.

Which there wasn't enough gold to physic a jaybird. But he got most of the town into his pants pocket."

"Why for? What was he trying to do?"

"I dunno. Just trying to run things, is how I sees it. Hell, it's his bank, his Drovers' Rest, and his helluva lot of everything else. He owns a lot of what people think somebody else owns, if you catch my drift."

"I do." Clint thought a minute. "A man like that, he always has to get more."

"How d'you mean that?" The cattleman was showing more interest suddenly.

"I mean he'll have to get more. It gets into the blood. For instance he'll be wanting a new marshal, but one under his thumb."

"That's why I bin speaking to you, Adams."

"Have you got a notion who he might have in mind?"

"I can say for sure it won't be the same feller I'd pick. Unless . . ." And the trace of a smile touched his eyes. "Less it be yourself. He'd be foxy enough for that."

"You were."

And suddenly they both laughed. It was a good moment, and Clint felt the ice had at least cracked.

"Well, whatever I told you, I'd tell him to his face."

They left it at that and finished their drinks.

Clint stood up. "I have one thing more to say, Casper. I'll be helping Norah Caldwell handle Knox Hollinger's business—that means his spread—till it's settled."

"I figgered that one out already," Casper said, getting to his feet.

"That means I don't need any help and for sure no company. I don't expect to see any of your riders on the R Bar O range."

The cattleman stood there, saying nothing.

Then Clint said, "I will be riding over shortly to take a look for any Bar O stock that might've accidentally got mixed in with 88 stuff."

"Then I'll be sending men to do the same, just in case there be any 88 in with yourn'."

Clint Adams gave a big grin at that, but the rancher was looking away. But only for a second or two. Then his eyes returned to the Gunsmith.

"Good enough," he said.

The Gunsmith nodded, and he walked out to where Duke was waiting for him.

As he rode away with the sun hot on his back, he realized that Chance Casper had looked again at his desk, at the framed photograph. Yet it had hardly even been a look; the moment was something that Clint had felt rather than registered through his eyes. Chance Casper had not looked at the photograph of the woman on top of his rolltop desk in the ordinary sense of looking; but something had gone out from him toward it, something invisible yet felt absolutely by Clint Adams.

He rode away thinking of that and thinking how it showed him a good deal of Chance Casper—something that was much more real than just description.

The sun seemed even hotter as he rode now, drilling into his shoulder blades and almost burning the backs of his bare hands, one of which was holding the leather reins, the other lying loosely on his thigh.

And he was no nearer to discovering who had murdered Knox Hollinger or why.

All the same, he had met Chance Casper, sized him, and been sized. Somehow the air had cleared a little. He was pretty sure it hadn't been Casper who had killed Knox—not personally and not through ordering—although it could easily have "happened" through the 88 Slash organization. A foreman or somebody wanting to get a good shine with the boss, maybe. Clint didn't believe that Casper would have directly ordered such a thing. Or would he?

It struck him suddenly that the picture on Casper's desk could have been somebody close but someone lost, someone who had perhaps died. There was that feeling in the atmosphere coming from Casper. Hard to define with words, yet it was there. No question. So that could possibly have been a motive.

Yet not for somebody who had died. But someone who was perhaps still living but ill—gravely ill, immobilized. Or was he just knitting his thoughts? Chance Casper was one tough sonofabitch. He'd had to be to build a spread like the 88 and to have gone through some of the things Clint had heard about: building his cattle empire, running everything, and expecting total agreement from everybody.

Except now. Now with Tennessee Fitz in the picture, it was abruptly different. Fitz was not only a competitor for power, he also controlled the bank. So that while not dealing as a rival cattleman, he was through the bank dealing very much with livestock. He was very much a competitor in Casper's own field. And not just a competitor but a threat.

Clint was satisfied that Casper wasn't wanting to control Little Horn—the cattleman would easily leave that to Fitzsimmons—but he did want to control the range around Little Horn. He always had, after all. But now he was being challenged by Tennessee Fitz. And Chance Casper was facing his toughest battle. A battle much tougher than those with the Kiowa, the Sioux, with the trail, with—yes—even the winter of the Big Die-Up, when the prairie had frozen solid, the cattle frozen with it, and the big dream had gone bust.

Clint had not experienced it personally, but he knew men who had gone through it. He saw what it had done to them. Especially those like Chance Casper, who had come through. The man was still a fighter, but he was getting older. And he was also being challenged by someone who didn't play by the old rules; the old rules, which didn't always play from honor—which sometimes were damn dirty; yet clean or dirty, the action could still be related to what a man might call "rules." Only now there was nothing that could be called "rules"—not even bad ones. It was a whole new game. It was, the Gunsmith realized, not a game at all. It was a war. A war with a smile on its face.

SEVEN

Dismounting, the Gunsmith squatted beside the dead Indian, looking for sign. He'd simply come upon the corpse when he'd stopped at the little creek to rest and water himself and Duke.

Shot in the back. Just like Knox Hollinger? Wondering, he stood up now and looked about. He looked at the scattered playing cards, then at the tracks of two horses—one iron-shod, the other without shoes, evidently Indian. And there were prints of a pair of range boots.

An Indian and a white man playing cards. Gambling, and that was a gut. He knew how the Indians loved to gamble. He wondered if they'd been playing cooncan, an Indian favorite, though certainly the game itself didn't matter. Well, it was as it was. Whites and Indians did gamble together, and not seldomly. He stood still, studying the scene.

An Indian and a white man. Gambling, for sure. And

the Indian shot in the back. He leaned down and turned the body over. A Shoshone, he was pretty sure. He squatted again and studied carefully, piecing together the story until he had a pattern. The Shoshone tracks and the white man's. It looked like the Shoshone had won—had probably stripped the man he was playing with—and begun to ride off. Carefully, he examined the prints, especially where the Shoshone had hit the ground. The impression was distinct in the soft ground.

"He must've been shot off his horse," he muttered, talking half to himself and half to Duke. "By the loser, who had a hideout, because the Indians usually play for everything —guns, horses, even women." Yes, that was the story. Each of the gamblers was alone. The action had probably taken place the day before.

The Gunsmith had been walking carefully about, knitting the story into a whole piece. Then, seeing something by a chokecherry bush, he squatted again, a low whistle escaping his lips. He was looking at a fresh print. A man had been wearing moccasins, and it was not the man who had been killed. Moreover, the tracks were fresh—likely from that morning. It was clear that pretty soon there would be visitors. It was time to get out.

At that point his eye caught the sparkle of reflected sunlight. It was an empty bottle of whiskey, and he judged it to be recent—very likely part of the gambling that had taken place. But now there was only the question of leaving quickly. He led Duke into the creek, then returned and removed any sign of their presence. At last, he mounted and rode down the stream of water till he found a bed of rock that they could get out on without leaving tracks. Then he cut for Little Horn.

On the high edge of a draw he drew rein, took out his field glasses, and looked back. They were there. He could see their movement, though blurred, through the trees. He considered himself lucky to have gotten away.

Shoshone. He wondered what band, who their chief was, and where they were camped. It might be a good notion to pay a visit. He thought it strange that the bottle of whiskey, though empty, had been left there. And it occurred to him that it might have been intentional. Not long after that, he considered the same notion about the killing: Had that been intentional too? Or was it really only a dispute over the cards?

The light was just leaving the high rocks of the long valley as Clint rode toward the R Bar O. He reminded himself that it was no longer Knox Hollinger's brand but Norah Caldwell's. And then too there was the Caldwell spread, also in the valley, which was under the hand of Tom Caldwell. Left by their father, the Quarter Circle C brand would be seen by Casper as partnered with the R Bar O. Prime range, on the edge of the vast Casper outfit, and a prime target.

The evening light was now soft on the land. The sun had settled behind the big rocks, and a slight chill was in the new air. It felt good to Clint after the day's hot sunlight, and he was looking forward to coffee at the R Bar O, plus the pleasure of Norah's company.

He had a lot to sort out. And there was also the question of checking the R Bar O stock that would have gotten mixed in with the 88, either through accident or design. He had told Casper that he could expect a visit.

It had been an interesting confrontation, he reflected now. He'd kind of liked the old buzzard. He knew the type: hard, raspy, cantankerous even, but the kind who let you know where they stood. Chance Casper was the type who had built the West and won the frontier, albeit not always through diplomacy and concern for the people they were dealing with. The West was tough, and the men who challenged it had to be even more. Like Casper. Clint Adams didn't agree with a lot of it. Yet he had left the boss of the 88 knowing that, within certain boundaries, he could be trusted. He didn't see Casper as a back-shooter, for instance. He might be a man who'd order a beating or two for an offensive person but not a cold killing. He didn't engage in out-and-out rustling, but like any stockman of the time and place, if a few head here or there happened to get mixed in with his brand, they were offered hospitality. It was what was done. Everybody branded slicks. But Clint Adams didn't see a man like Casper using a running iron to actually change a brand. And the current way of it was that if somebody else's brand got mixed in with yours, you let it be. If the beef's owner came by and found it, then it was a mistake, an accident. It worked both ways from the middle, as the oldtimers put it.

In the shadow thrown by the edge of a steep draw, he drew rein and let his eyes cover the terrain ahead and also behind. He had all along been watching his back trail carefully, mindful of the possibility of pursuit by the discoverers of the Shoshone's body.

At the same time, it had occurred to him in the

period following his departure from the dead Indian that there was something that didn't quite ring right about the whole scene. It was plain that a white man and an Indian had been playing cards; there had been a dispute, and the Shoshone had come out second. It was also evident that there had been drinking. The evidence was there: the bottle, the cards, the tracks of the horses and participants in the drama. There were also the tracks of a second Indian, who had apparently discovered the killing and, Clint presumed, gone to spread the tale.

Then why wasn't he satisfied? He just felt that itch; something was not ringing true. Yet what was not true? The man was dead; there was, after all, a body. He had been killed recently. He had been shot in the back, and that was what had killed him. He didn't have any other marks on him. He hadn't been choked to death, for instance, and then shot. And anyway, why would someone want to do that in the first place? What would a setup like that serve?

No, it was a typical scene. He knew that those Indians who gambled usually bet everything. And there was the evidence that the winner had started to ride off on his unshod horse, leading the other animal, which was shod. But he—the Shoshone—had then been shot, very likely with a hideout. That was surely the reading.

Everything fit. And yet he felt that scratching, that nagging that something was not quite as it appeared. He was, in other words, missing something.

The bottle! Why had it been so far from the dead man, from the place where the game had taken place? Wouldn't it simply have been dropped when it became empty—near the cards, in other words, which were also spread out?

The cards! Why so spread out? If there had been a fight —and there were no signs that there had been—then the cards would have been all over the place. But had the cards and the bottle been thrown about *after* the killing?

He felt something quicken inside him. And if the cards and bottle had been staged, then why? Somehow, as he kicked his horse forward, he knew that something wasn't right. The Shoshone had been murdered, but not as a result of a game of cards. But why?

In the twilight he came over the low lip of land below which lay Knox's spread, the three-room cabin built of green spruce logs, with spruce chinking on the inside and clay outside. The roof was sod. From the thin chimney came a string of smoke, rising into the dying light. And there was the barn, also spruce, but in this case not peeled, roofed with sod, the grass on it growing high; the chinking here was manure. The round corral was built of more spruce, with pine posts.

The whole outfit lay in the bottom of a bowl. The Tensleep River ran by thinly at the eastern end of his vision, a meadow leading up to it. As Norah had told him, the place had been a line camp for the 88, where cowboys wintered, keeping the river free of too much ice for any stock drifting that way, while also watching out for young stuff lost in storms.

Clint had really been taken by the meadow when he'd first seen it, and this time he was even more struck, in the soft twilight, by the sense of peace and silence that it gave him.

Duke shook his head suddenly, his bridle clinking, his mane tossing. A bay horse—it looked like Norah's —at the hitching rack nickered low, then, sticking out its foreleg, bent to rub its nose alongside it.

When Clint rode in the door opened and light poured onto the stone slab that lay in front of the wooden doorstep. Then Norah blocked it out.

"I was hoping it was you," she said, and he heard the happiness in her voice.

"Are you alone?"

"Tom just left. He stopped over to say he'd be by in the morning to help us check stock if we needed him. But I told him we'd come over there."

"He's not here now?" Clint asked, wondering at his good fortune. For the moment she had opened the door and his eyes had fallen on her, the moment he'd felt her atmosphere, smelled her—whatever—his passion had swept through him like a tornado.

"I was hoping to meet Tom," he said, "but I'm glad he's not here, to tell you the truth."

"Would you like me to tell you the truth?" she asked, stepping back from the door so that he could enter.

"I reckon I do. If it's good," he added with a grin.

"I reckon it is," she said, imitating him. "I mean by that, podner, that I mean to say as how I be glad likewise that Tom ain't hereabouts."

He had kicked the door shut, and he put his arms around her while they laughed together.

And then he was fondling her, his tongue deep in her mouth, his hands pressing her buttocks against him.

"The door!" She almost gasped the words, tearing away from him and locking it.

He had unbuttoned almost half the buttons that ran down the front of her calico dress, and as she came to him, he slid his hand inside.

"I could hardly wait for you to get here," she said.

He had his hand on one of her high, firm breasts, and she murmured her joy.

Then he took her hand and led her into the bedroom. In a moment they were both naked and he was kissing her body, as she moved slowly to sit on the edge of the bed. Then, taking his erection in her mouth, she felt his balls with one hand, while the other hand held his buttocks and pulled him closer. Not that he needed to be pulled.

"I don't want to choke you with it," he said.

"I'd be very happy if you did."

She was on her back then, with her legs up on his shoulders, and he mounted her, pushing gently into her wetness, riding her with long, tantalizing strokes, slowly, very slowly, and then gradually increasing his tempo, while she held his balls, playing with them. Their tongues licked and sucked together. Stroking in perfect unison now and only increasing their speed slowly, then one or the other slowing a little to delay it a little bit longer . . . tantalizingly . . . impossibly . . . and yet with the absolute sureness and knowledge of perfectly matched lovers. Until neither could stop, or change it, or do anything but obey that law that was greater than themselves or any human who ever existed: the law that rode them, drove them to their utter desire, their complete abandonment and climax.

They lay together, arms and legs still locked, gasping, totally complete. There was not a single thing in the entire world that either of them could possibly want. They had it all.

That night they took it all again. And again. Neither kept count, for it was not the amount of times that mattered but something quite else, something beyond either of them. Certainly the Gunsmith knew it was beyond him, and that was all he could deal with. That power that swept him and the girl into extinction; that supreme joy of dying and living totally at the same time.

The next morning they were up in the predawn, and while Norah was still getting dressed, Clint built a fire in the range and put the pot on to boil coffee.

"I'll get some breakfast," she said, coming into the kitchen, while he took a good moment to admire her looks.

"I wouldn't fight you if you wrangled us up some eggs and biscuits."

"Sure will." She stepped quickly toward him and, stretching up a little, kissed him on the mouth.

"I'll take a look at my horse," he said. "Then maybe we can wrangle the six you got down in the breaks."

"You want to do that before we ride over to the 88 to check stock?"

He nodded, heading for the door. "Like to know where everything is when we meet up with Casper's boys and maybe have to talk business. Fact, I'm not so sure about you coming along."

"Nonsense." Her tone was firm, and he saw there was no point insisting. She could get into just as much trouble staying back here at the outfit, with maybe some randy boys riding in while he was away. Besides, he wanted her around when her brother was there, so the three of them could work out their strategy.

Duke was standing outside the barn door, which gave into the round corral. Seeing Clint, he nickered.

"Looking for some oats, are you, lad?"

His tone was easy, but he was alert all through his body, just in case any of those feisty 88 boys should take a notion to pay another visit. Norah's bay horse was inside the barn. He forked some hay and poured oats. Then he took a walk around the spread, checking for any strange tracks, but found nothing out of the ordinary.

Norah had everything on the table when he got back to the cabin. "I see somebody taught you how to cook up a pot of arbuckle all right," he said as he took a drink of coffee.

"*Arbuckle*? You mean *coffee*?"

"Right. That's what they call it in the trail camps. At least now and again. It's good," he went on, "no matter what you call it."

It didn't take them long to finish breakfast, and then he went out and saddled both horses. By the middle of the forenoon they'd wrangled in the six head from the breaks, leaving them in the round corral, with access to the barn. Then they headed toward the 88 range.

It wasn't long before they spotted a few head grazing in the hot morning. Mostly 88, but there were two R Bar O.

"We won't cut 'em out right now," Clint said. "I just want to get a rough tally before I talk to anybody."

There were more cattle down by the wide creek. Again the 88 brand was dominant, but there were six of Knox's.

Now the day was so hot the sound of the heat crackled in the trees and the dry, almost brittle grass, and it hit a man in the face like limp leather. Everything was hot to the touch—the saddle horn, his thighs as they spread across his saddle, the butt of his handgun. The sun burned into his back, it scorched; and for the pair of them there was no escaping it.

He looked across at the girl who was riding abreast of him. Her face was set, yet serene. He could see how hot she was, but she didn't seem to be perspiring much. Women were often like that, he had noted: more able to handle the heat than men and usually not succumbing to disarray. Especially the pretty ones. He wondered if that were really true, but then he tore his thoughts away from her as they drew farther into Casper country.

The horses had moved slowly across the prairie, their coats sleek with sweat. Twice Clint had stopped so they could dismount and rest their animals. But by noon they had tallied quite a few head of R Bar O stuff—mostly steers, but some she-stuff too and a few calves.

"I think we picked the right time for this," Norah said after one of their rest stops and they were in the saddle again.

"We'll have some figures to confront Casper with, and then we can take action. I figure—course, if you agree—to give him the chance to get out of it. I think he got what I was saying at our meeting."

A couple of times Clint had roped an animal out of a bunch of stock so he could read the brand up close for any running-iron work.

"Somebody's been painting pictures," he said now. "I've noticed a few others that suspicion it."

"Mr. Casper is not going to be very happy when he hears of his men's poor handiwork," the girl said wryly.

"That is for sure."

Of course, he knew they were being watched as they got closer to the 88 Slash. He had spotted outriders early on. Every so often one would show, just to make sure that Clint and the girl knew of their presence.

Clint had also picked out a Deane & Adams from Knox's guns when the girl had shown them to him, and now he slipped it into his shirt front. He had on a large hickory shirt, good for the purpose of concealment.

They were just topping a rise that looked down on a creek and the big Chance Casper spread when the horsemen came pounding up. They were again six—like the last time at the 88 Slash ranch house—and they were heavily armed, and they came in fast.

The Gunsmith simply drew rein and sat his horse. Norah followed suit.

It was Burt Clancy, the foreman of the 88 Slash, who kicked his big dappled gray ahead of the others.

"You're on Mr. Casper's range, Adams."

"And so are a lot of Hollinger beeves. I'm making a tally, and when I am finished I'll talk to Casper."

The foreman was shaking his head even before Clint had completed what he was saying. "No. You get off 88 range. I am saying right now."

Clint had already turned toward Norah, and now he pointed off to her left. "I believe that's about where your brother's at, miss." Then he touched the brim of his hat with his first two fingers, signifying that this was where they were parting, as obviously prearranged.

It was done so smoothly, and the girl responded so perfectly on cue, that she had turned her horse and was cantering off before Clancy and his men could react.

Turning right back to the foreman, Clint cut Clancy right off as he started to speak. "No one will need to go with her."

Clint Adams had moved his arm about an inch closer to his right hip, while he watched Clancy's eyes flick.

"No need to get yourself nervous, Clancy," Clint went on conversationally, with an easy smile, while with his left hand he reached for his chin and scratched. But he had drawn the attention of the group of hostile men to the gun at his side.

"Just don't get no closer to that .45," Clancy said. "There is six of us, Adams." The foreman's face creased in a tight smile around his cold, bullet-hard eyes.

"That is what I know, Clancy; and just like last time, I can hit you right in the belly, no matter how fast your men are. You figger that's a good swap?"

The foreman's small eyes dropped to the Gunsmith's right hand. It was just as Clint had planned it.

And with the speed of something that many men had termed quicker than light, the Gunsmith's other hand—his left—flicked inside his shirt and was out and up with Knox Hollinger's Deane & Adams.

"Right now!" And that gun was pointing right at the foreman's heart.

Burt Clancy's eyes flicked to the right and left of the Gunsmith, then looked beyond him. "I got men all around you, Adams. Right and left and back." His voice was tight as a drumhead.

"I know that, Mr. Clancy. But I don't need anybody

right and left and behind you. I've got you right here in front."

"I can order them to kill you."

"Mister, it seems to me we've been through this before. This time I'll let it be a dry-draw; next time I wouldn't count on that if I was you. Now then, I'm going to be calling on Casper. You can tell him I'll also be inspecting his herd."

"Clance . . ." The voice came from Clint's right. "There's a rider, two . . ."

"There are three riders," Clint said. "And they're coming from the direction of the 88. Spotted them a while back, Clancy. Your boys don't notice much, do they?"

"That could be Mr. Casper."

"Then we'll wait till he gets here. Save you giving him my message."

He sat quietly on Duke, taking out a quirly and lighting it one-handed, not for an instant diverting his attention from the 88 riders and their foreman.

In another few moments the rancher, flanked by two of the three who had shown up at Knox's place, rode up on a brisk little buckskin.

"What the hell is going on here!" The voice was hard, the jaw hard; the man's entire body was like leather and iron. He looked to Clint Adams as though he were about to ride that buckskin right through a stone wall plus three barbed-wire fences.

Nobody said anything. It was a harsh moment that should have wiped out any possibility of silence, even though nobody spoke.

At length Clancy said, "We caught him checking out

88 stock; him and the Caldwell girl. And he pulled a gun on us."

"Jesus Almighty! An' it's maybe too damn bad he didn't use that gun on yez! Cannot you knotheads do anything like I tell yez! Christ Almighty! One man and six of you-all! An' twice! And what girl? Where she git to?"

Clint was grinning. He had slipped the Deane & Adams back into his shirt.

"Rode over to Caldwell's place," Clancy said.

Clint saw that Jake and Chuck, who had shown up at the R Bar O with their sidekick Lolly, were watching him closely. Chance Casper was still cussing. Clint noted that the rancher, like most of the old cattlemen, was not packing any hardware. Damn few of the oldtimers did, knowing that only a fool would throw down on any big man. Doing such a fool thing would only rouse the community to a lynching.

"You men get back to work," Casper said suddenly. "Clancy, I will see you later. Take these two peckers with you." He barely nodded toward the pair who had accompanied him.

Then he was facing Clint. "Like to have a word with you, Adams. Tear yourself away from your beef tally for a minute and come take some grub. It's 'bout that time." Squinting up toward the sun, he kicked the buckskin into a trot.

The Gunsmith was smiling as he followed suit. Somehow, there was something he liked about Chance Casper. That old buzzard was a slicker, and he could swipe the shirt off your back without you even getting out of your coat. He was tough, mean, ornery, selfish, and totally used to giving orders and pushing people about. He ruled his acreage. He was not at all like those big oldtimers—at least some of them—who reigned during their declining years. Not at all. Chance Casper didn't reign; he ruled.

Clint Adams liked that. True, he would never have agreed with ninety percent of a man like Chance Casper. He had fought such men in the past, and he probably would again, as now. Yet, somehow, he had been touched by the man. Was it the photograph he'd seen him watching during his last visit? He wondered.

It was the middle of the afternoon by the time he left the 88 Slash. The dinner he'd shared with Chance Casper had been a good one. Filling; and the rancher had brought forth the splendid accompaniment of a fresh bottle of whiskey.

They had talked all through the meal. That is to say, the rancher had done most of the talking; and Clint had certainly let him, for he was after information. In fact, he had said so.

"I am going to find out who murdered Knox Hollinger," he said, just after they had seated themselves at the table and the manservant had disappeared into another room.

"I would like to know that myself, Adams. I want to say this, before we go any further: You likely'll be surprised to hear that I backed Hollinger's getting into office. I talked with him when he was sent out here. And the point is, I'd asked for the law. You might think that funny."

"Why would I?"

"Why? On account of most people think Chance Casper figgers he's a law unto hisself."

Clint laughed appreciatively at that. "Well . . . ?"

"Well, as you see, that's very probably so. I do things my way. Like any man with guts and good sense who's ridden trail all through this here country—and I am includin' Texas, by God. Places where there wasn't no law. A man carried the law on his hip. Hell, Adams, you understand that."

"I do. But there is still the law back of the badge."

"Lotta people in this country figger that tin for a likely target."

"Tell me what happened to Knox. I'd heard he was going after a bunch of rustlers'."

"Far as I know, that was so. See, about two, three years ago, there was a rumor about gold being in the country; up around Bobby Creek. Exceptin', it proved wildcat. Not so. Somebody thought there was a lost mine—and who ain't heard of dozens of lost mines in this country? And when that proved a fluke—meaning nobody had a notion of where the hell it could even maybe, possibly be, let alone actually was—then it died down. Things died down. Only next thing, somebody claimed there was another one, up around where the Stinking Water comes down and forks off into the Little Stink River. Anyways, that proved wrong too." He paused for a drink, then leaned back, gasping with pleasure, his tumbler nearly drained.

"So how did Knox get into that?" Clint asked. "Is that what you're leading up to?"

"It died down, but the mob that had come into town on the rumors and stories didn't die down. Fact, it got even bigger. The damn town was like Dodge, Abilene, like any of them hell-on-wheels towns the railroad dropped everywhere they got to. You know what I'm saying."

"Real pleasant spots. I do know what you mean."

"Fact, when I first discovered Fitzsimmons was in town—see, I don't get into town a whole helluva lot anymore—but still, not never. Still, now and again. Well, I heerd Tennessee Fitzsimmons was in town, I thought, shit, by God, we're done for!"

"How so?"

"You know how Fitzsimmons was in that big bustout down to Crow Creek when he shipped in one of those hell-on-wheels towns which he brought in on the railroad."

"Sure, I know what they are. I've been there. But I didn't know about Fitzsimmons," Clint said.

He remembered well the hell-on-wheels town, though not at Crow Creek. But he had been at Quicksburg when a long train of flatcars had rumbled into the station, with every car loaded high with knock-down buildings, storefronts, dance-hall floors, tents, wooden sidings, and entire roofs and porches. And with all this there immediately followed the populace —saloonkeepers, gamblers, restaurant impresarios, road agents of every kind, and, of course, the whores and their consorts. The settlements were made of highly perishable materials —canvas tents, turf houses, cheap lumber shanties—which, as the railroad moved on to its next camping site, were all pulled down and sent forward to the next "town"; or, if in too wretched a state of disrepair, they were simply abandoned as worthless.

These rough and temporary towns were simply stopovers for the people building the railroad, laying track; and as Clint had seen, there were no places more corrupt, ugly, or dangerous. He remembered now that it was at Julesburg where he had first heard of Tennessee Fitz, who was famous as the entrepreneur of these ghastly towns, so aptly named hell on wheels.

"I see what you mean," Clint said now, bringing some of the scenes he'd witnessed back through his memory. "And you figured when Fitzsimmons came to Little Horn, he was going to build it up like one of his hell-on-wheels towns."

"Something like that." Casper nodded, reaching now for his box of cigars. "Something like that," he repeated.

"But he didn't."

"What did he do?"

The rancher opened the box and offered Clint a cigar.

"He didn't do that," Casper said. "He made himself to home right in Little Horn, and next thing anyone knew he'd taken over the bank, the Drovers'—well, he had that moved up here from Laramie—some of the saloons, restaurants, and God knows what else. For all I know, the sonofabitch likely owns the cemetery." He reached for his glass.

"But you're figuring he isn't through," Clint said, studying Casper's face for a reaction.

"I'm figuring somehow the sonofabitch hasn't even begun."

"How's that?"

"I dunno. He is just too damn quiet. I mean, except for the pressure he is putting on me to get out. Sell! Christ almighty!"

"That is a tough one," Clint said, and he meant it. For there was nothing slimey about Chance Casper. He was one tough sonofabitch, for sure; but he was somewhere straight. The men who'd come after the cattlemen were tough too, but they hadn't worked with their hands. Not a one of them had ever ridden night herd, handled a stampede, or fought the Indians, drought, storm, and all the other natural disasters that came from working stock or the land. The new men dealt with cards, documents, promises, and money. Lies.

"That why you wanted Knox Hollinger as lawman?"

Casper nodded. "He was a good man, Hollinger. Ornery, course, but a man who seen the straight of things. You seen what he got for his pains. Damn them! God damn them!"

"*Them*? Who?"

"Them!" He stood up, walked to his rolltop desk, and stood right there, looking down at the picture. "Them! The bastards who come in and took over with their paper and shit. Cost me a fortune for . . . for my family." He was looking into the middle distance, his cigar in his hand.

"Family?" Clint asked.

"That's Miriam." He was speaking with his eyes on the photograph. "She's been in a place. I go see her. She don't know who the hell I am. Me! We was together fifty years near. And she don't know me."

"Where?" Clint asked. He stood up and walked over to where Casper was standing. "Where is she?"

"Denver."

Clint looked at the young woman in the photograph. She was looking wistfully at whoever it was had taken her picture. Clint Adams thought she was beautiful.

"She is a beautiful woman," he said.

"That is for sure what I know," said Chance Casper.

"But it's costing you a fortune to keep her where she is."

"My daughter's there. Lives in Denver and visits. I go every now and again. But I got to keep things going here. Got busted all to hell with the big Die-Up. It hit real hard around here. Reckon you know that, Adams. You put me in mind of Hollinger."

"He was a friend of mine."

"When you was siding the law?"

"Yeah."

"Think over my offer. I'll pay you well. I can still rustle up something."

"If I ever pinned on tin again, it wouldn't be with some private citizen paying my salary," Clint said.

Casper said nothing. He walked back to his easy chair and sat down. After a moment, Clint followed suit, figuring it was about time to leave but realizing, too, that the subject of misbranded cattle and even the presence of so many R Bar O stock mixed with the 88 Slash had not been mentioned. He decided it was time to get down to the nub.

"I tallied a goodly number of R Bar beef mixed in with your cows," he said abruptly.

The rancher didn't even look up. Plainly, he had been elsewhere. "I'll have the men cut 'em out, Adams. You know, I wish you'd study my offer. You don't have to run for the law. I'd hire you as a regulator. A bodyguard. A private detective. Whatever would cover your feelings on the situation."

"Tell me what it is you want," Clint said. "But first, it's agreed—right?—that no matter what I answer to your proposition, your men will cut out R Bar O stock from yours, starting tomorrow."

"Agreed."

"Shoot, then."

The rancher had been looking across the room, his eyes squinting, as though coming to some decision. For a moment he didn't say anything.

Clint reached for his cigar, which he'd placed on the ashtray that said it had belonged to the Denver House. He took a luxurious pull on it. It was pure Havana, and there were not many things that he considered equal to a good cigar.

A moment passed. Clint looked over at his host, wondering for an instant whether he had fallen asleep. But it was not so.

Chance Casper took a pull at his drink, then reached for his cigar. Looking at him, Clint thought how he seemed almost to have aged, even during the time he'd just been with him. He watched the cattleman who had once been one of the biggest in the Wyoming country as he took a pull on his cigar.

Chance Casper blew a cloud of smoke toward the ceiling. He seemed to straighten in his chair. His face seemed suddenly different—even, Clint thought, younger. His pale blue frontiersman eyes were on his guest.

He said, not taking his eyes from the Gunsmith, "I want you to kill Fitzsimmons. I will pay you whatever you ask."

EIGHT

Clint Adams got a good kick out of reading the local newspapers, wherever he was. Not the big stories, necessarily. The out-of-the-way items, the gossip, the local color vignettes always gave him what he appreciated more than bald news: that is, the taste of a community, the sort of atmosphere that made a town, an area, what it was in its own unique way. He knew from experience that it was in throwaway material that he could sometimes find something important. A bit of gossip, a joke that somebody told; something not made much of, hardly noticed, but that now and again fit into his own tapestry of thought. He thought over his meeting with Chance Casper and the cattleman's somber though radical request that he kill Tennessee Fitzsimmons. The important "bit" he realized he could easily have overlooked was the fact that the rancher did not actually want Fitzsimmons killed but was rather expressing his own wish simply to be rid of the man.

For Casper knew that the Gunsmith was not for hire. He'd been told as much, and firmly, by Clint. Yet, this—the removal of Fitzsimmons—was the one thing he wanted more than anything else.

In this he revealed to Clint his innate simplicity, but also his inability to deal with such a complicated type as Tennessee Fitz. It had been quite a revelation for the Gunsmith to suddenly see so starkly the limitations of Chance Casper: that he was no murderer. He could kill, certainly, and he had killed. But in hot blood only; or so it seemed to Clint Adams.

Well, the Gunsmith had walked away from it. He had ridden over to the Caldwell spread and found Norah and Tom together. After an hour's visit, during which they discussed how they would check the stock, Clint left for town.

He left with a good impression of Tom Caldwell. A few years older than his sister, he yet relied a good deal on her innate common sense. It was pleasant for Clint Adams to see them together. There was affection there, without a trace of sentimentality. He rode off with the feeling that Norah had good protection with the young, broad-shouldered, and intelligent Tom Caldwell.

But he still had no inkling of who had killed Knox Hollinger or, really, why. Of course, in a general way, it had to be somebody who'd felt threatened by the marshal of Little Horn. Or—and this sudden thought was unexpected—had it been somebody from "before Little Horn"? Someone from the past, maybe getting even for something? It was a thought that only just then occurred to Clint, for he'd been so wrapped up in the action in Little Horn with Casper and Fitz and even the crazy carnival with its mad leader, the Reverend whatever-his-name-was, that he'd concentrated wholly on that area for an answer. And so he'd tried to think back to anything Knox had dropped in his presence or anything he'd heard elsewhere concerning his friend that would lead to something suggesting a motive for revenge. But nothing. Nothing whatsoever came to mind.

And he was back to his earlier conviction that it had to be something to do with the current situation in Little Horn. Only, what was the situation—the real situation—in Little Horn?

And he was back to his newspaper, letting his thoughts, his feelings, play on the gossip and news of the town. As printed in the *Little Horn Truth Teller*. Again he was finding how relaxing it was, whenever he came to some problem such as the one confronting him now, to simply let his thoughts float while he did nothing but allow the play of suggestions, facts, ideas, and even daydreams take over, like a stream in which he could simply be still and watch; whenever something surfaced, he was there to catch it.

Seated against the back wall of the Hot-Shot Saloon and Recreation Parlor with the *Little Horn Truth Teller* open at the front page, he read with relish of the scene that had transpired right in front of him at the Great Caravan of Mystery. He'd been there in person the last time he'd been in town, and it was especially enjoyable to read about it now in the paper, for he could linger on it more than had been possible during the actual event, which, to be sure, had been gripping. And then, the accomplished writer—who was nameless—had written his story as though it were actually happening right now. So Clint had the satisfaction of recalling nearly all of what he had noticed himself, the news story bringing it all back intensely. . . .

"Step right up, ladies and gents, and get your two-bit bottle of Dr. Orton Prouty's Famous Dosage and cure yourself and your loved ones of whatever ails them!" The medicine hawker was a knobby little man whose sharp elbows pushed against his tight frock coat, his knees against his stiff pants. He appeared to be made of corners. He had the habit of spraying those nearest him with liberal doses of saliva; at one point during his exhortation he became so excited over his fabulous product that he nearly lost his teeth, grabbing them in the nick of time before they would surely have fallen onto the platform or maybe even among the front row of awestruck listeners.

"Ladies and gents—noble citizens of Little Horn, the heart of the Great West—this miraculous mixture is known all over the Great American Frontier as the People's Choice! It is without any question whatsoever the great family medicine of the age—or any age!" he added, his enormous forefinger held high, a sword cutting into the past and future. "Taken internally, it is guaranteed—I say *guaranteed*!—to cure burns, the cholera, swelled joints, boils, ringworm and indigestion. It will literally wipe out asthma, consumption, bronchitis, wasting of the flesh, whooping cough, and night sweats. It will equally cure the illnesses that attack a horse or a dog. Children love its taste. It will rejuvenate those parts of the older anatomy that require it—eh!" This brought a titter of laughter and here and there a male guffaw from the crowd. "Made of pure vegetable compounds!"

He was a marvel. He spoke without stopping and, what was more, without repeating himself. And as he spoke he even illustrated certain illnesses and physical problems: the aching back, the asthmatic weeping, a hacking cough, a limp, a pain obviously in the groin—though because of the presence of ladies, he did not emphasize the point or even mention it as such.

They loved it. They stood with their mouths open, their hands moving toward their money belts and their purses.

Clint had been standing beside the little old man and his burro in the front ranks of the crowd. He was in a perfect spot not to miss a word or a gesture; and also, it turned out, to catch the whole action of the little old prospector.

"I will take a bottle of that there," the old man said. He was small and thin; the seat of his baggy trousers looked as though he were carrying a bindle in his crotch. When he opened his mouth, his aged breath laced the surrounding atmosphere with a mixture of tobacco, booze, and rotting teeth. Yet Clint had spotted a glint in the old boy's eye. He was the first customer at that particular show as he tossed a coin to the medicine man.

The old boy was clearly closing on eighty, Clint figured. Although his clothes were ill-fitting, they were patched. Clint received the curious impression that it wasn't that those garments were too large for him but, rather, that he was too small for them.

The hawker handed down a bottle of Dr. Orton Prouty's Famous Dosage, while at that very moment the burro standing beside the old man suddenly knelt down, then rolled over to lie on its side. The crowd swiftly moved out of the poor animal's way. A murmur rose from the onlookers while, indeed, the hawker of Dr. Prouty's Famous Dosage gaped. But the old prospector never turned a hair.

"Old Annabelle, she can't handle all that fancy talkin' stuff," he said. "An' anyways, she does have a touch of the croup." He uncorked the bottle and, kneeling beside his burro, pulled back her lip with his thumb and poured.

"Annabelle, I reckon you need this here more'n myself."

And lo! Annabelle twitched, flicked an ear, rolled an enormous eye, and rose. With a helping hand from the old man, she regained her feet, acknowledging this great event with a reverberating bray that almost brought the assemblage to its knees with delight.

"Praise the Lord!"

Suddenly, and to the utter astonishment of everyone present, the voice of the Reverend Crispus Quinn gripped the throng. "The Lord has delivered this humble beast of burden from the jaws of death! The Lord be praised! I say, THE LORD GIVETH, AND THE LORD TAKETH AWAY! And by God, He has sure given us back this noble animal! An animal—a beast of burden, yeah!—who has served its master well!"

"You hear that, Annabelle?" shouted the old man, shouting because of the din that had ensued as the Reverend finished his speech.

"Remember, everybody, there will be services tomorrow morning in front of the large caravan. All are welcome!" The Reverend turned toward the old prospector. "And you, sir, bring Annabelle to our flock!"

Clint was watching the scene with total fascination, and he took particular note of the unctuous tone, the oily gestures, of the self-appointed Man of God. He didn't know that the Reverend was reveling in one of his best roles—indeed, his favorite, next to, of course, that of lover.

Finally, Annabelle and her owner, after purchasing two more bottles, ambled off, while the crowd all but besieged the hawker for Dr. Prouty's Famous Dosage.

The phrase, oft-repeated, was clearly the hawker's favorite, for he delivered it with his whole self; and it seemed to Clint especially effective with the extra-ordinary cerise bow tie that bobbed up and down on his generous Adam's apple as he spoke. It appeared to Clint Adams that it was there not only to give emphasis to his words but to agree with him.

Adroitly avoiding any contact with the Reverend Quinn, the Gunsmith slipped away from the scene. Now, enjoying a beer in the Hot Shot Saloon, he lived it all again in the *Little Horn Truth Teller*.

Then, all of a sudden, it hit him like a thunderclap on a calm night: What in the name of Jumping Jehosephat was a *prospector* doing in Little Horn!

"You have got to remember," the Professor of Games and Gambling was saying to half a dozen "pupils" who had signed up for a course in "Curing the Gambling Habit"—under the direction of Professor Folio Throckmorton—"that about eighty percent of all cardplayers are stupid. They are plumb dumb," he went on, "as the old sourdough put it. It's easy enough to see that is so if you just watch things."

Clint had paid his admission money out of sheer curiosity and, of course, also in the hope that he might get a line on some of the things that were obviously taking place in Little Horn. A town reputed to be as bare of gold dust as the middle of the Atlantic Ocean: so why the old gold-panner and his burro? The fact was clear that somebody believed he might strike it rich in the territory. In fact, Clint had heard some mutterings in the saloons and in the crowd that afternoon.

The professor, however, now called his attention and everyone else's in the room that had been hastily thrown up from the supply of lumber and other building materials brought in with the Great Caravan of Mystery.

"See," the professor was saying to one of his pupils, "you just made a dumb play there. You had kings up and you were sitting to the left of the opener and didn't raise. Figure! Kings up can be topped if too many players stay in. Think! What if there'd been three, four hands who stayed after the pot opened? Your hand was good enough for a call, but it was not good enough for a raise. Once a greener stays in, it can be a helluva wrangle to drive the bugger out."

The group of six players was listening carefully to everything the professor said and really hanging on his words.

"Suppose you have aces up," the professor continued, "or kings, queens, or jacks up, and you're sitting close to the opener's left: Then you ought to raise. I say you 'ought to.' You *should*!"

"What if you're raised back?" a young man asked,

with the firm tone of voice implying that he had aced the professor.

A rich chuckle bubbled out of the professor's loose lips. He had been just waiting for that question. "If you're raised back, you fold your hand, or else you reraise and hold. Course, then you got to bet following the draw, and you hope the other man don't call."

"Why?" the same young man asked, scratching the side of his big jaw.

"On account of he raises before the draw he's more'n likely showing your two pair is dead."

"But how about two small pair?" the young man insisted, and Clint realized he was a plant.

The professor shook his head. "They're not worth playing unless you raise before the draw and stand pat, then bet. You got no more chance than a fart in a windstorm of making a full house there, my lad."

The professor, rich with victory, paused, taking a cigar from his breast pocket and lighting up.

"Never stay on a short pair," he said, his voice sonorous with the authority of the ages. "Never stay on less than two kings or aces."

A sigh ran through his vigorous frame, and the plume of smoke from his fine cigar rose royally to the ceiling. "Lookey here! Suppose I'm sitting on the opener's left; I raise, then, on aces or kings, but never in the same pattern." He released another smaller cloud of smoke, sniffed, then resumed.

"And don't be so all-fired quick to open if you happen to be sitting close to the left of the dealer. If you got a strong hand and someone ahead looks like he'll open, pass. See?"

"Why?" another player asked.

"So's then you can raise when it gets back to you."

He beamed upon his little class, all of whom had paid well to join. And, of course, Clint knew that he wasn't the least worried that any one of those present would remember what he had taught a week from then or would even be able to apply it. To be a gambler, you had to be a gambler—blood, bone, and breath.

"Remember," the professor was saying, "we're talking straight draw. You practice this."

Clint had really been enjoying himself. But the best was yet to come. The professor dealt it like the professional he was.

The young man at whom he had directed his last injunction to practice now asked a question: "Can you teach me how to deal seconds?"

A strange look passed swiftly across the professor's face as he collected the cards. He surveyed his pupil as though he had suddenly realized his question. A long silence fell, while he built the cards back into the deck, shuffled, cut, shuffled, and then slapped the deck down on the baize-top table just near his own hand.

The young man had not been prospering in the lengthy silence, and he was beginning to fidget. Clint wondered if he was the law; so, obviously, did the professor. But it was not likely, looking back on the way the young man had handled his cards, that he was anything but what he appeared to be—a hayseed.

Finally, after an endless silence, the professor spoke, his words falling like pieces of ice.

"Young man, if I was a bit younger—just a bit, I say—I would take you outside and whip your ass into a more becoming way to address your superiors!

"Hell, I was only askin'! Hell, anybody who's any good deals seconds!"

"Anybody who is any good, young man, *can* deal seconds," the professor said, correcting with professorial aplomb. "If he should wish to," he added. "But a good player does not have to cheat." His sharp eyes surveyed his recent pupil through a haze of cigar smoke, and Clint suddenly realized he was the man in black he had seen at Knox's funeral and whom he'd pegged as a gambler.

The young man's face was reddening quickly now.

The professor tapped his middle finger on top of the deck of cards. "What a man who wishes to gamble needs to know is simply this: How to watch. Watching is everything. Remember that, when you play poker or any game, you aren't playing cards, you're playing the other players. And for that you need three things." He held up his thumb. "Number one: vision." His forefinger came up next to his thumb. "Number two: clear thought and common sense." His middle finger sprang up beside the other two. "Number three: patience!"

He lifted his cigar, took a luxuriant drag on it, and watched the blue smoke drifting upward. "Class is dismissed." And then, cocking an eye in the direction of Clint Adams: "If you want to sign up again, see the clerk out there."

It was just then that Clint Adams recognized who he was looking at.

"Long time," the professor said.

Clint nodded. "You give 'em their money's worth, Horace."

"Always did, my friend. But, uh, the name is not

Horace. It's Obediah—Obie, for short—Turpin. Professor Turpin." He grinned suddenly, and Clint noted that the grin made Horace Lejeune, sometimes known as Ace LeJeune, ten years younger.

"It's been a while," the Gunsmith said. "But you didn't come to town with the Reverend, and you shaved since I saw you at the funeral."

"The Reverend and myself are old acquaintances." The man whose name was now Obie Turpin touched the corner of his mouth with his finger. "You're still Clint Adams, are you? You're still the Gunsmith?"

"I'm still Clint Adams—Ace." And he watched that reminder sink in for "Professor Obediah Turpin."

When the Gunsmith picked up his room key at the Drovers' Rest, the room clerk behind the big desk turned out to be a woman he had never seen before. He was pretty sure she was wearing a wig, but he had no doubt that the down on her lip was indeed a mustache. For a moment he wondered wildly if it were actually a man in disguise. But, surveying, her ample figure, he realized it was not so. A bona fide woman, with more than just the suggestion of a mustache, a resonant voice, yet with a big bust, which she leaned gratuitously against the edge of the desk; black, liquid eyes, a painted mouth, and a lot of paint in her eyebrows, which seemed almost lacking in hair.

"I'm standing in for himself," she said, evidently catching Clint's surprise, which he hadn't tried to conceal. The woman was obviously quick.

"Glad to meet you. I'm Clint Adams."

"I know that." The voice was strangely soft. The big

head nodded in the direction of the stairs. "You got company."

"Oh? Mind if I ask who?"

The Gunsmith's sense of humor was not lost on the lady with the mustache. "Good question. Your friend Kelly. I sent her up, so's she wouldn't catch so much attention like if she was setting around down here in the parlor."

A strange voice, strange accent, somewhat cultured and also not.

"What's your name?" he asked, suddenly realizing he didn't know.

"Louise."

"Louise?"

"The Louise."

"I reckon by the way you put it that there is only one."

"If you reckon that way, Mr. Adams, you would be wrong." She sniffed, rubbing the end of her stubby nose with the palm of her hand. She was wearing several rings and a number of clinking bracelets. "My first name is Theodora—The, for short. My second name is . . . ?" She raised her eyebrows and her forefinger, pursing her lips a little like a schoolmarm quizzing a not-too-bright pupil.

"Uh, Lily Langtry?"

"Smart aleck." Her scowl barely covered the humor that was ready to break through. But she held it. Instead, she said, "I run the house down the end of Main Street, and I haven't seen you about. Howsoever, our girls manage to get around, I'm happy to say. I recommend Kelly."

"I'll take your word for it," Clint said agreeably, the laughter pushing at his eyes. At the same time, he realized that nobody was getting away with anything in Little Horn.

At that point the regular room clerk walked in.

"What have they got for soup at the O.K.?" Louise asked.

"No soup. Mulligan stew is what I had." Skinnegan, the room clerk—apparently a man with no given name, because nobody in Little Horn had ever heard it—stepped behind the desk, slipping past the large figure of Louise with some difficulty.

"The lady is my wife," he said to Clint, speaking formally. "Which is why I now and again invite her to hold down the desk while I go for coffee or something to eat."

"I see. Well . . ." He turned to Louise, who had come out from behind the desk and was now standing with her back to the big picture of Tennessee Fitzsimmons. "Nice meeting you, The."

"Everyone calls me Louise," she said amiably. "Even the most intimate, and even the least. Nobody, not even him"—she threw a thumb in the general direction of Skinnegan's bald dome—"calls me by my first name."

"I see," the Gunsmith said, though he was not sure whether Skinnegan was a first or last name either. It sure didn't matter, in any case. He would not forget this interesting couple very quickly. "Did you know Marshal Knox Hollinger?" he asked suddenly.

Skinnegan suddenly began to cough, and Louise sniffed. "Everybody 'round here knew Marshal Knox," she said, her eyes thoughtful. She looked quickly around the lobby, which was apparently deserted. "The marshal was well liked by some and not so well liked by others, if you catch my drift."

"I do," said the Gunsmith.

"But you are a smart one, I can tell. And I have heard tell about you, mister. I can only say this: Little Horn is the kind of place where a person wants to keep their nose clean."

"You took the words right out of my mouth," the Gunsmith said. He gave a nod and started to turn toward the stairs. "My company alone? Or am I being nosey?"

"She is alone." The humor was all gone now.

Clint found her sitting on the edge of the bed when he walked in.

"What I like about this place is the privacy," he said:

"I couldn't help it." She had risen the moment he opened the door and now stood in front of him, with her hands at her sides and a resigned expression on her face. "Louise is . . . well, she has her own way of doing things, and she has to do what she's told to."

He had shut and locked the door. Now he stood facing her. "Who tells her?"

"I don't know. I—I wish I'd never started this."

"What do you tell them when they ask you about me?"

"I told them I like you, and I think you're a very nice man. And then they say, Do you want anything to happen to him? And I say no, and then they say to keep seeing you and let them know if you say anything."

"Like what?" He had sat down beside her on the bed now and was searching her face for sincerity. He was pretty sure she was being straight with him.

"Like what you're doing here."

"But they must know that. I have said it around town: I'm going to find out who killed Knox Hollinger. That's no secret."

"I know. They told me that."

"So what else?"

"I guess they hope you'll say something; maybe something you don't intend to say. Like they ask me if you are connected with anyone else. Did someone send you? Are you working for the law? Things like that." She suddenly put her head in her hands. "I told them I don't want to do this. And they said it's too late."

"But who? Who is 'they'?"

"First it was Louise. Then it was a big man with a red face. I don't know his name, and I've never seen him before or since. Then two men—also whose names I don't know. One of them was tall and thin, the other just sort of a regular size."

"Were they packing guns?"

"I didn't see any. They were the ones that really scared me. Especially the tall one. He mentioned my sister. See? Oh, I am frightened! I don't want any of this."

"What did he say about your sister?"

"He—he just asked me how she was." She put her head in her hands and started to cry.

He continued to sit beside her, thinking. Clearly, whoever was in back of things was someone with a lot of power. He knew the kind. The kind to whom people owed money, the kind who gave favors and withheld generosities, the kind who could fix troubles and thereby ensnare loyalty.

"Did anyone ever give you money or lend you money to help your sister?" he asked.

She looked up, letting her hands fall into her lap. He saw that her eyes were red, though she still looked good, even with all the sobbing. Even though he wasn't thinking of her in that way right now.

"The man at the bank loaned me money. Or, that's to say, the bank loaned it."

"Who was that?"

"I don't remember his name. But I owe them a lot. And . . . and, yes! Now that you bring that up, Louise said something about money I owed. She didn't mention the bank, but she said it was known around town that my sister needed care and that I was in debt. Big debt. Louise said it. You see, it wasn't said bald like that. Do you know what I mean? It was pointed out, like."

"I know. The iron hand in the velvet glove."

"The *what*?" But then she said, "Yes! I see what you say there. That's a good way to put it." For a moment he saw her as a child who had discovered something.

"They've been using your sister—Muriel?"

"Millie."

"To get you to work for them. That's one thing that is for sure."

She said nothing, continuing to look at him.

He was sewing it together, looking into a corner of the room as he spoke. "Someone wants the power in this town; someone who's already got a lot but wants more. That means he's got to have a whole lot of help. But he's smart, this fellow. He doesn't come out like, say, a Jesse James or a Sam Bass, putting himself on the line. No. He's more like that feller Plummer, up in Virginia City. The sheriff of Bannack and a whole lot else, but at the same time he's a man running the road agents and killers. Respectable on the surface, but underneath a killer. Our man's like that. He—probably like Hank Plummer—he'll have a whole network of people helping him—people who owe him for favors, people he'd helped, people whose secrets he would know. A great big spider web with himself at the center, pulling the strings, building his web."

He said it half aloud, thinking it out along with the words, speaking half to the girl, half to himself, his eyes still in the corner of the room.

"Aren't you forgetting something?" she asked suddenly.

He turned his head and looked at her profile, for she was also looking across the room, speaking as though feeling for the words. "Aren't you forgetting that I'm supposed to be working for them and telling them things that you say?"

"I haven't forgotten for a minute," he said. "You can tell them every word I said if you want to."

He reached over and took her hand.

The room was small, but the bed was wide: Clint took note the moment he walked in. They had agreed to meet separately at her place. It was a small cabin she shared with her sister, Millie. Millie was out, as it happened, and in the small room that was Kelly's, the dying afternoon light washed along the cheaply constructed wall.

Clint didn't care. She had locked the door after them and turned to him. His arms slid around her. She was crying, but he felt it had to be tears of relief, actually. In fact, it was how the girl put it as they lay down naked.

"O God, I can't believe I'm here," she said softly.

"I'm so happy. So happy! I've been wanting you so much."

"I'm glad," he said, pushing his erection between her thighs. His body was raging for her, and he could tell she was experiencing the same hunger.

Yet they didn't hurry. They took their time, playing gently, teasing and licking and kissing and stroking and hugging, deeper and deeper as they continued the beautiful ritual. She had a lovely body, with high, firm breasts, the nipples long and hard now with the passion that was wrapping itself with his. Her bush was spongy with its delicious wetness, and her aroma filled him with even more excitement. She rolled on top of him then and slid down. His rigid organ popped up under her chin, and then her tongue was licking it and finally sucking it, deep into her mouth, down her throat. Long, slow, timeless sucks, until he thought he would lose all sense of where he was.

Then suddenly, but without the least rushing, she had turned and was facing his feet, his organ still in her mouth but now with her hairy bush right in his face. He licked her soaking lips, eating her deliciously, while she did the same.

It lasted forever and at the same time for only a moment, and they came together gloriously, choking each other with their love juices.

They rested, neither speaking, lying on their backs close together and holding hands. Presently, as though by some signal, each knew the other was ready, and as one body they began again to stir, roused by the single passion that ruled them, drove them to the utmost delights. He mounted her high and deep, and together they rode their shared passion to its ultimate and wholly exquisite destination.

Now they lay there panting.

"Oh God! I knew you had a big one," she said.

"And I knew you had a tight one."

"We seem to be well matched, wouldn't you say?" she whispered, reaching down with her fingers to tickle once more his resting organ. For the moment he was spent. Or, rather, he had thought he was; but her fingers knew no denial. And almost immediately, his manhood began to grow again until it was as hard as ever.

"From behind this time," she said.

The Gunsmith said nothing. He was beyond speech as he stroked into her soaking, quivering vagina, even deeper and higher than the time before. And they came like this, with him riding her from the rear, until they both collapsed in total joy and exhaustion.

Then they slept.

Next, Kelly said, "Let's try it face to face this time."

"Any way you like I know I'll like," he said.

"We seem to have the same tastes," Kelly said, tickling her tongue in his ear.

"I think you taste real good, young lady."

"I think you taste real good."

"Let's try some tasting then."

"Let's try everything," she whispered.

"I think that's a great idea," the Gunsmith said, as their bodies began to accelerate. "It's the most fun you can have without laughing, somebody once told me. An old man," he added.

But she wasn't listening. She was beyond listening. And now so was he, as their bodies sealed themselves together, only parting slightly and in rhythm as was necessary for the proper, most enjoyable strokes that now mastered the two of them and once again swept them into total, utter, and unbelievable oblivion.

NINE

The morning light was dancing through the recently washed window of the office of the Eastern-Western Land Company, situated quietly apart from Little Horn's main street. The separation of the small building from the rest of the town had been intentional. Mr. Robert Fitzsimmons, president of this seemingly simple organization, was seated in his copious leather armchair, his feet up on the edge of his desk, as he enjoyed his first cigar of the day.

Tennessee Fitz always enjoyed the early hours, not that he was by any means a lover of nature or especially wished to witness the rising of the sun; rather, he favored the absence of people. Alone, he could do his thinking, planning, organizing. For his large head buzzed almost continually with plans. He was a man who dealt with the big picture as well as the smallest detail. Moreover, he loved his work. He loved himself; that is, the picture he held of himself. And indeed, it was this noble picture that he claimed to represent—the kind though tough, alert, cultured, honest, and upright servant of the people and lover of all mankind; not to forget the champion of Manifest Destiny and the winning of the West. In fact, he had contributed ably to the conquering of the frontier, as the military picture on the wall of his office attested. Or it was supposed to. It was the same picture that hung in the Drovers' Rest: the staunch leader; the far-seeing eyes probing the horizon for further conquest, the chest high and firm, ready for more medals; the man who had annihilated the band of Chief Singing Rain and paraded his victorious soldiers and their trophies—scalps and other parts of the conquered savages' anatomy—in the big theater in Denver.

His eyes now fell proudly on the victorious man in uniform who seemed to return his look, a look that penetrated the man sitting in the easy chair: the eyes, the brow of a conqueror, an even-handed administrator of the future of a great and mighty land. The savage frontier tamed!

Of course, he had enemies. What great man did not? His friends, partisans, and followers were legion! That small band of carping critics, drenched in their jealousy and envy, were still bringing up stories to the effect that he had massacred a band of peaceful Indians, mostly women and children with not a firearm among them! And a band, moreover, that was flying the Stars and Stripes on the chief's lodge!

Nonsense! Lies! Didn't they claim the same thing about Custer at the Washita? The jealous fools.

And now there were those who were trying to oppose him in time of peace—trying in Washington, in

Cheyenne—to deny his heroic, patriotic efforts to civilize the West: land for farms, homes for families; the great railroad that was spanning the entire continent and opening the West to the civilization of the East!

His cigar had gone out, for in his daydreaming of his great achievements, both past and future, he had lost himself completely. As he frequently did. No matter! Taking out a match from his coat pocket he relit, then resumed the careful detailing of his Great Plan, from which his dreaming had stolen him a moment earlier.

At which point there was a knock at the door, and when he called "Come!" Stamper, one of his trusted men—an "inner circle" member—entered.

"The Reverend Quinn has come, sir."

The man in the deep chair pursed his lips, as he reached to his waistcoat and took out his gold horologe.

"Good. He is on time. Time, Stamper, as I have often told you and the others, is what makes the world go round. Without time . . . where would we be? Eh?"

"Lost," said Stamper, a man in his middle years with a grave demeanor, a scar along the left side of his face, and very big shoulders.

"We'd be out in Poker Flats in a shit storm, that's where we'd be, Stamper! Without even a compass or a prayer. Look at this country!" His thick arm swept the room. "What has a man got here? Without his limits, his territory, his land with a house on it, and a plough and team of horses! I ask you! All he can do without what we're bringing him is set on his ass and look farther and see less. Eh, Stamper!"

"That's right, Mr. Fitzsimmons."

"You bet your ass it's right, Stamper."

A cough suddenly rumbled up from his chest and he was at once overcome, hacking and spitting into the spittoon by his chair, then wiping his face with the big handkerchief he had dragged from a pocket. At last he subsided, while Stamper waited.

When he put the handkerchief away—it was actually a large brown bandanna—he picked up his cigar, sat back again, and put his feet up on the desk.

"You want me to tell him to come in?" Stamper had shifted his weight from one foot to the other, a movement that was not missed by his employer.

"Not yet, Stamper. Let the Reverend wait a bit. You see, here again, time is important, Stamper. You understand? The longer a man—an impatient man, such as Quinn happens to be—I say the longer he has to wait, the less he will be in control of himself. And the surer he'll be in the control of . . . well, let's just say somebody else."

Stamper said nothing.

"Stamper, do you understand?"

"I do, sir."

But at that point there came a loud clearing of the throat outside the still-open door and the visitor—the Reverend Crispus Quinn—appeared.

"Ah, Reverend!"

"Mr. Fitzsimmons!"

The greetings could not have been more cordial.

"Stamper, bring coffee. And, er, perhaps something to go with it. Eh, Reverend? I've got something right here."

"I'd be happy to join you, sir," said the Reverend, his unctuous tone riding calmly through the buccaneering camaraderie of his host.

He sat down, as Tennessee Fitz straightened in his seat and, with a flick of his hand, dismissed Stamper.

When the door was closed, there was a small moment of silence. This was ended by a whistling sound coming from the Reverend's false teeth as he opened his mouth to speak and smile at the same time. His host, meanwhile, slapped his big palm down on the top of his desk and cocked an engaging eye at his visitor.

"I think we're in," said the Reverend.

"Not quite. Not quite. But close, my lad," said Tennessee Fitz, noting from the corner of his eye that the rising sun had now caught the glass covering the large picture of himself in his military uniform, looking out into the distance of the future that was just waiting to be conquered.

"Well, you made it!"

"That we did! Fitz, you're looking great, my lad."

"I can say the same for you, Crisp. And by God, we'll drink to it."

Tennessee Fitz reached down, opened a little door at the bottom of his desk, and pulled out a bottle and two shot glasses.

"It's early, but I've already said prayers," the Reverend declaimed sonorously.

"Tell me when to stop," Fitz said, pouring.

"When you get to the bottom of the bottle."

This brought a rich chuckle all 'round.

Tennessee held his glass high. "A toast."

"To the enterprise!"

"To the Eastern-Western!"

"To those noble men who brave storm and Injuns and dishonest lawmen, bringing the distilled wisdom of centuries in brown-liquid form to support the efforts of the heroes who are subduing the wilderness, the wild savages, and those sonsofbitches who stand so unwisely in the way of Progress!"

"Reverend! That is the one." Tennessee Fitz was beaming. Yet it was still necessary to go one better.

And so, just as the rim of his glass was about to touch his lips, he said, "And to the swift and frequent consummation of our desires!" He drank quickly, concluding the toast before his visitor could top him.

Lowering his glass with a sigh of pleasure, Tennessee Fitz regarded the Reverend with a smile. "I do want you to know, Crisp, how much I appreciate your sending the countess to me. I do believe I can help her with the land problem she's finding herself in."

The Reverend smiled, looking as though he'd just received an overflowing collection plate. "Good. Poor young woman, she was quite distraught. And I couldn't resist. After all, it's my calling. I took pity on her."

His host smiled back at him, looking as though he'd just swallowed a gold canary and thinking, I'll just bet you did! "Why not drink a toast to the countess then?" he said, raising his glass.

Lowering it—empty—he said, "Good then. I have some things I wish to discuss with you, Crispus."

"And I with you," said the Reverend.

But before either could say anything further, there came a knock at the door. It was Stamper, with coffee and some biscuits.

"Every foreign laborer landing on our shores is valued—economically—at $1,500."

Tennessee Fitz read from the government report he was holding before his pleased eyes. Raising those eyes now, he looked over the top of the paper at Crispus Quinn. Then he lifted his eyebrows in pleasure. "He rarely comes empty-handed. The superintendent at the emigration depot has stated that a careful inquiry produced an average of a hundred dollars, almost always in coin, as the money property of each man, woman, and child landing in New York." He lowered the paper to his lap and reached for his drink.

"You see where that puts us, Crispus."

"On Easy Street."

"Not quite yet, my friend."

"Of course! I am not a fool, Tennessee! What do you take me for!"

Tennessee Fitz was pleased to see that the booze and hospitality were working. "I apologize," he said. "Crisp, you know I didn't mean that as it sounded. Why, man, I depend on your acumen, your good old hoss sense every step of the way. But I am only cautioning that we don't start counting chickens before they're hatched."

"Of course, Fitz, of course."

"My friend, we are in this together."

"I have never supposed otherwise," the Reverend said firmly, in a clear clerical tone, as though someone had questioned Scripture.

"I'm just touching some highlights now from the meeting in Cheyenne," Tennessee Fitz said.

"And Chicago. Don't forget."

"And of course Chicago. I hadn't forgotten!" But he was pleased to notice that Crisp Quinn was getting a bit agitated. Which was the way he wanted him: just a bit off balance. Thus, he'd let the lead slip more and more into his own much more capable hands.

"In Chicago, Crisp, Arthur Hoskins, just back from Washington, was arguing in favor of more government grants and construction funding for more railroads across the West, claiming that in less than a dozen years the railroads would attract enough immigrants to put nearly five billion dollars more into the country's wealth. How do you like them canned peaches, my friend!"

"I like them peaches fine!" Crisp Quinn's face was wreathed in smiles. "But how are we doing in the way of getting immigrants is what would be good to know."

"All that is being handled by men skilled in their particular art. Kensington, our main contact in Washington, and Rolfe, our man in New York, have worked together in perfect timing to spread the news in newspapers all over Europe. They're calling America the cornucopia of the world.'" He reached to his desk and picked up a newspaper. "Listen to this: '. . . flowery meadows covered in nutritious grasses and watered by crystal-clear streams. Two million acres of farming land!' My friend, every day new agents are being dispatched to Europe armed with posters, circulars, and lantern slides."

"Slides!"

"Slides." Tennessee Fitz literally smacked his lips. "They are overlooking nothing in the way of getting our material about. They put it in schools, consular offices, railroad stations, aboard ship. Everywhere! Also in English, French, German." He paused, lowering the paper he was reading. "I can tell you, Crisp, that we—Eastern-Western—have distributed hundreds of thou-

sands of maps, circulars, and even a company maga-
zine."

"And I presume the returns are good. I mean by that,
that many immigrants are still coming."

"The other land companies are doing it too," Fitz said.
"Sending out literature and overseas agents."

Fitz nodded. "This is especially true where you come
in," he said.

"I am more than happy."

"As a rival."

He watched the Reverend's finely chiseled jaw drop.
"A rival!"

"Look, there are boatloads of them coming. I mean,
our agents have been selling land to the immigrants all
over Europe. They are presently pouring into New York,
the gateway to freedom, liberty, free land—"

"*Free land*? Did I hear you say *free*?"

"I should have said free homes. The idea is that in
human nature there is a basic desire to get something
for nothing."

"I'm certain most people know that, Fitz. But of course
. . . of course." He sat back—he had been on the
edge of his seat—and scratched the side of his long
nose. His forefinger brushed some hairs protruding
from his nostrils. "Yes, of course. They will do
anything—anything at all—to get something for
nothing. Well, I am with you. But what do you mean,
rival?"

"I mean just this. For example, there are right now
some three million acres owned by the railroad. That is,
at this moment. We—Eastern-Western—are not in
the business of transportation, but we are selling land.

Now then, the government, generous as it is, does not feel too happy about one or even two or three people controlling all the land. You understand? It gives a bad name sooner or later."

"Makes it look like somebody's getting greedy."

"I must say I admire the way you put that!" They both chuckled.

"So we will continue," said Tennessee Fitz, "as though we are in different areas. We don't even know each other. If anyone gets close, we're actually against each other; we're rivals. You get me?"

"But of course," said the Reverend, who was ahead of it. "We can drive the prices up or down as we wish."

"As, uh, Eastern-Western wishes," corrected Tennessee Fitz.

"But of course . . . but of course!"

Wreathed in smiles, the two drank each other's health.

"By the way," the Reverend said, "I wonder if you've heard about the Mennonites." He watched Fitz carefully, having saved the juicy tidbit for the precise moment. Which might be now. And it was. He saw the other's eyes tighten.

"What Mennonites? They a country, some place in Europe?"

"They come from Russia. The Crimea. I have this on the best authority."

"The best?" repeated his companion, cocking a wry eye and grinning.

"Straight across the baize-top," said the Reverend. "Thirty-four, maybe thirty-five families just got to Kansas. They brought gold out of Russia with them and they have bought up eight thousand acres from the Santa Fe.

They have put up a row of A-frame houses in a mile-long street, set about a hundred and fifty yards apart. One for each family."

"That's money in somebody's pocket."

"Not in the Mennonites' pockets. But there are more coming."

"Well, it's what we've been talking about, isn't it? It's what we're here for."

They fell silent, each savoring thoughts of money and power. *Rivals!* each was thinking. Rivals to the public, but privately controlling the market. Working, as it were, in tandem.

"You will see an attack in the *Little Horn Truth Teller* tomorrow," said Tennessee Fitz.

"An attack? On who?"

"An attack on the Great Caravan of Mystery."

"What the hell you getting at?"

"The next issue will publish an attack on the National Association of Undeveloped Land. That is me. But without my name, of course, appearing. This attack will be by you. I have already written it. It's here for you to read and sign."

He could see that Crisp Quinn didn't like it. But it was the only way. The time had now come for his ace. He knew Quinn's weakness; and so he led right to it.

"I'll have to read that pretty damn close," the Reverend was saying.

"Of course. But of course! By the way, I understand you've gotten nowhere trying to hire Adams's gun."

"Have you?"

Ruefully, Tennessee Fitz shook his head. "I'd say it was getting to be time to get rid of him. I've a

strong notion he's here in Little Horn following up on
Hollinger. I mean, he's been asking around about him.
Claims he's going to find out who shot the marshal.
They were old friends, it appears. So he could be on
the same mission—same job as Hollinger. You have
surely figured that."

"I surely have. What's your point?"

"My point is that it's time for something to be done
about Adams. Like time he found out who killed Hollinger."

"Or who ordered it?" Crisp Quinn added slyly.

"Someone might have to take care of Mr. Adams."
Tennessee Fitz cocked his head to one side and pushed
his tongue into his cheek as he surveyed the Reverend.

"Man who'd take Adams—the Gunsmith—would
by damn get quite a reputation in the West. In fact, all
around the whole country. Probably get books written
about him. The fastest gun ever—faster than the famous
Gunsmith even!"

He watched his words puff the man who was listening
to them with the most avid attention.

"He'd have to be a real good man. Real fast, to
be faster than the Gunsmith! What a hero! Wild Bill
Hickok, move over. Eh!" Tennessee Fitz rumbled out
a very appreciative laugh at what he had just said.

The Reverend Quinn was cogitating, as he put it to
himself. It was something he'd come to a while back:
the need for the execution of the man known as the
Gunsmith.

And at the same time there was another question, a
question that had not been raised. True, Maritza had

been mentioned at the start of the conversation; Maritza and the section of land left her by her late husband, which had been proving troublesome to her.

"What about Maritza?" the Reverend asked suddenly. "We need to go into that. I thought you might be able to help her, with your many connections."

"I told her I would look into it," Fitz replied, with swift ease, though caught suddenly off guard.

"The land, as I reckon it, is up around that feller Casper's outfit. And I heard he'd been having trouble with Hollinger—or was having trouble—over something or other."

"Over graze and water rights, very likely," Tennessee said, recovered now and speaking smoothly. "Glad you reminded me again. I'll look into it. And, uh, let you know."

But Crisp Quinn hadn't been raised on the riverboats for nothing. He took pride in his perceptive abilities. And he took especial pride right now, for by damn, the talk that had been in Tennessee's hand for most of the discussion had now fallen into his. He could feel the change in atmosphere. Ah, it was good. Nothing like the cards and dice to teach a man how to catch a slicker. And that Fitz was a smooth one. By damn he was holding something up his sleeve. His silence on the subject had given him away.

Well, he would question Maurie when he saw her, but carefully. He knew how. He knew her weaknesses. And by damn he knew his own. That was the big thing in dealing with people: to know your own weakness. He wondered if Tennessee Fitz knew his. And for a flash he wondered, too, if that sonofabitch sitting there all smart-alecky, like he'd just swallowed the Great Key to Salvation, had been in Maurie's pants.

Clint had just walked into the O.K. Cafe for a cup of coffee when he noticed the old man sitting in the corner. It was the prospector he'd spotted at the Caravan of Mystery, the old boy with the burro who had bought a couple of bottles of the hawker's medicine.

The old man was just leaving. He was old, all right. Clint figured him to be in his seventies. But like all those oldtimers, he was a tough one. There was a glint in his eye as he didn't return Clint's nod on the way out.

Then Felice came in to take Clint's order, and he thanked her for having tipped him off about the Casper men whom he'd escaped that day. When she came back with his coffee, he asked her if the three men who'd followed him had given her any trouble. She said no. Everything had been all right.

She had walked over to clean up after the old prospector and was chatting with Clint over her shoulder when suddenly she stopped, with an exclamation. He looked over. She was staring at something on the chair where the old man had been sitting.

"Come! Take a look at this!"

He stepped quickly across the room.

"What can that be?"

Clint was staring at the seat of the chair, almost as surprised as the girl.

"What is it?" she said again.

"It's gold dust." He reached down and picked some up with his fingertips.

"It must have spilled out of his pocket."

"That's what it looks like, doesn't it?"

"Where is that Emile? He's supposed to be here! That lazy . . . What if I'd come on that alone?"

"Or what if someone else had?" Clint said calmly.

"What do you mean?" She was looking at him in surprise.

"I mean, you'd likely be in the middle of a gold rush." He stepped to the window. "Did you notice which way he went?"

"No. You mean there's gold! Gold about here somewhere?"

"I don't know. But I'm going to find out. Now listen, clean that up. Do not tell anyone about it. Not anybody. Understand?"

"Not even Emile?"

"Not even Emile. Please. Listen to me: That can cause a panic. People can get hurt. Just keep it to yourself until I find out what's going on."

"But if there's gold—"

"If there's gold we'll all learn about it soon enough."

"But why not now?"

He had walked to the door. "Please, Felice. Do what I ask. It might not be a real strike at all. It might be too soon to say anything. Because if word gets around, there'll be a stampede. I've been in one of those. People get hurt. And it could also be a mistake, and then you might find yourself in a riot. People could get badly hurt," he said again.

She was staring at him, her dark eyes very round and very large. She was holding the knuckles of one hand against her mouth.

"Did you notice which way he went?" Clint asked again.

She thought a second, then said,. "Yeah. I think I saw him crossing over. He might have been heading to the Pastime for a morning stiffener."

"I'll come back. I'll let you know what I find out. But keep quiet about it."

"I will."

And he knew she would.

He had decided to head for the Pastime, but then all at once his attention was diverted by a big wagon unloading in front of Cratchett's General Merchandise & Hardware Store. Something attracted him, and he paused, his thoughts still on the old prospector and the gold dust found on his chair.

He was remembering how at the Caravan of Mystery, listening to the medicine man, he had wondered what a prospector could be doing in a place like Little Horn, where no one had reported even the smell of yellow dust within a couple of hundred miles. More. And for sure, if there had really been a strike, the old prospector wouldn't be hanging around town. He would be out staking a claim as big as he could handle, at the same time keeping his mouth shut.

He wondered if anyone else had thought it strange having a prospector in town, burro and all. And he wondered, then, how long it would be before another sign was left pointing in the direction of a strike.

On the other hand, if it wasn't fake, well, maybe there was something real going on. The best thing might be to mosey over to the Pastime to have a closer looksee at the old boy. Maybe even get him into conversation. Buy him a drink or two.

At that moment his attention was drawn again to the men unloading the wagon outside Cratchett's store. And then all at once he saw it. They were unloading shovels, picks, and axes. A lot of them.

TEN

The old prospector, as it turned out, had not gone into the Pastime. Clint Adams, crossing the street after spotting the shovels and picks and axes being unloaded outside Cratchett's store, had entered the Pastime and, not seeing a sign of the old man, had decided to leave. Just then he was caught by a voice behind him.

"Clint Adams! By God, it's been awhile!"

Turning, he saw the vague figure emerging from the dim corner of the room. The first thing that struck him was the fringed buckskin shirt the man was wearing. It had a beaded design on the front of it and was obviously a special garment. Clint had only seen one other like it in all his years in the West.

"Virge Mulholland," the voice went on. "Dodge."

"I do recollect," Clint said, as the figure became more clear. And it all came back to him. Dodge City, with Masterson and the Earps and Luke Short. The whole bunch had been there. And Virge Mulholland.

"Buy you a drink, Adams?"

"I wouldn't say no."

They were moving toward the far side of the room, away from the crowded bar.

"Grab that table there and I'll collect it," Mulholland said.

While he was gone, Clint studied the room. There wasn't a face he recognized, though he was sure that a good many of them knew who he was.

And Mulholland? Pretty far from his usual ground, it seemed. The man worked mostly with the stage lines and railroad, although the company wasn't averse to spreading out into other areas when necessary.

Mulholland's appearance came at an interesting time, for Clint had been getting a strong, rapidly growing feeling that the Little Horn situation was beginning to move—that something was not only opening up but coming to a head.

Virge Mulholland, with his guttered face, thick mustache, and big hands, was approaching with a bottle and two glasses.

"So, what has brought the ace of the staff to Little Horn?" Clint asked in a low voice, as the tough, bandy-legged man approached. He'd been careful not to even whisper the name Wells, Fargo. Nor had he forgotten the time he'd seen that leathery man with the nut-colored face and watery eyes cool Big Billy Brocius right in front of an angry mob lusting for Wells, Fargo's guts.

Mulholland sat down, tipped his hat brim up with his thumb so that he could see the room better, and lifted his glass of whiskey, which the Gunsmith had meanwhile poured.

Presently, after sampling the whiskey, smacking his lips, and building a smoke and lighting it, the Wells, Fargo agent decided to answer, although in keeping with the Westerner's method of indirection.

"I have heard that one Knox Hollinger caught lead poisoning and got himself planted."

Clint gave a slight nod, almost imperceptible.

"The office figgered it might be time to have a look-see on what's goin' on around Little Horn. I recollected you used to know Hollinger back in Dodge and around, an' when I heard you was in town here, I mentioned it at the office. Thought you might be about and could give me a hand."

"Knox was working with Wells, Fargo?" Clint deliberately kept the surprise out of his voice, even though he'd asked a question, for he felt the need to play it very carefully.

"No. Not exactly. I wouldn't say that," said Mulholland. "He was like maybe onto something that could've had a bearing on the company. And we got wind of it. That's how come they figured to send me along. Then, course, when we got wind that Hollinger had been kilt . . ." He sniffed, blinked, and reached for his glass, removing his cigarette and breaking what was left of it between his thumb and finger and dropping it to the floor.

"The company doesn't miss much," Clint observed wryly.

"I have also been picking up on that yellow stuff that some folks call gold."

"Funny you mentioned that," Clint said, and he told him about the old prospector.

Listening, the Wells, Fargo man built another smoke, Clint noting how swift, clean, and wholly accurate his movements were—and without a pause between reaching for his makings and the first inhaling, leaving the cigarette hanging on his lip as he spoke.

"Burro and all, huh? D'you reckon he's in cahoots with those carny people?"

"Could be. The feller who runs the carnival looks to be a mite too sharp for a reverend spreading the Word about." Clint took a drink and continued. "I met him, and I have seen the most of his operation—pet bear, fortune-telling, palm-reading, snakes and wild animals like a tiger, juggling and pistol-shooting. I am told the Reverend sees himself as an ace with the .45, and that when he isn't in his church rig he's popping around all duded up in black, with silver-handled six-guns on each hip; all black, right down to the underwear and stockings, I have been told."

"A gunman," said Virgil Mulholland laconically, and he squinted past the string of smoke coming from the cigarette that hung so casually from his lower lip. He canted his head in the direction of his companion.

"It looks to me like we both have the same question," Clint said.

"Who killed Hollinger?"

"And why?"

Clint said, "There is the question of gold, and like I told you about the shovels and axes and all that I saw being unloaded in front of the hardware store."

"You figger that caps it."

"I am wondering if there really is gold or just a fake alarm."

Mulholland inclined his head. "I bin studying that, too."

Then Clint told him about the dead Indian, the empty bottle and cards, and about the tribes getting whiskey.

They were silent with this for several moments, each turning it over carefully.

Finally, Clint said, "There is also one of the big outfits run by Chance Casper trying to spread out but being hog-tied some by the bank and a feller named Tennessee Fitzsimmons."

Mulholland nodded. "The Eastern-Western Land Company. That's him. Looks like we're steppin' in it for sure."

"You know Casper?" Clint asked.

"Not personal. Heard of him a good bit. Tough old bugger, but, well, dunno how square."

"Fitzsimmons has got him over a barrel," Clint said. "And Casper, he is desperate."

"Man generally is in that position," Mulholland said dryly.

"Casper is desperate," Clint repeated. "Fitzsimmons wants his land."

"How come?"

"I am wondering if maybe it's gold," Clint said, thinking of the old prospector. "Only somehow, I do feel it's not that."

"Something else maybe?" Mulholland had cut his eye sharply at the Gunsmith.

"Not 'maybe'. I'm almost damn sure. The gold is a feint."

"Feint? What the hell is that?"

"Making a move to catch you off guard, then coming

in from a direction you didn't figure on," Clint explained. "Like a dodge."

"Huh." Mulholland sniffed and then again. "Huh." He wagged his head. "Feint. Interestin'." He tossed his cigarette into the spittoon near his feet and followed up with a jet of saliva.

"I think we're talking about railroads and land sales," Clint said. "And I am wondering whether a gold strike would be a good or bad thing for Little Horn. And whether there really might be gold hereabouts or if maybe it's a dodge."

"Huh." Mulholland had taken out a wooden match and was now picking his teeth. "How close have you got to them fellers? Casper and Fitzsimmons, I am meaning."

"No problem there," Clint said wryly. "All I have to do is stand still."

Mulholland's wide mouth twisted at that. He reached up and adjusted his hat, then rubbed the end of his nose with his palm.

"Wells, Fargo is concerned about the murder of Hollinger," he said.

"So am I," Clint said dryly.

"Hollinger wasn't working directly with the company, but they were like working together. See, there is a lot of close talk about the railroad coming through here. Now, if the land companies can get enough immigrants to sign up, then the railroad will put a line through to Little Horn and farther, more than likely. Get the story?"

"But Casper's in the way of the plan. His land, that is," Clint said. "And Hollinger's outfit, too. But Casper wants that land independent of any railroad."

"I doubt Casper even knows about the railroad and

the Eastern-Western Land Company," Mulholland said.
"The company is not concerned with the railroad or the
selling of land to immigrants anyway. They're concerned
with Hollinger's murder."

"Why? He was a United States marshal. Why isn't
the government concerned? Why Wells, Fargo?" The
Gunsmith brought that question straight out and into the
other man's dark red face.

Virgil Mulholland was picking at his teeth with the
wooden match as he weighed that question.

"And there is also the question of the Shoshone," Clint
continued. "I have heard talk all around that there are
elements here and in the government who want their
reservation moved. It all seems to be homing in on either
gold or land-grabbing, or maybe both."

"Maybe both," said Mulholland, nodding a little.

"But where is Wells, Fargo in all this?"

"Adams, maybe I got to take you into my confidence.
I got to trust you."

"No you don't. And I don't give a damn whether
you do trust me or not. I know Wells, Fargo has got
to be involved if the railroad comes through here. But
why hasn't a new marshal been appointed? Where is the
government on this one?" He paused, took a drink, and
returned his glass to the table. "Of course, I can guess
that one. They did try to get me to take the job."

"The government?"

"No. Not directly."

"There could be people in high office working with the
land company. Eastern-Western, say. Or whoever."

"Tell me something new," Clint said.

"All right. Try this: The government *is* working on

it. They are concerned about the Shoshone. And they
know you're here. But they're not showing their hand
yet. There are big factions working with the railroad, my
lad. You saw what happened to Hollinger. That could
happen to you. You could already be targeted."

Clint nodded. "That's what I know. And I've got a
notion who is behind it. I mean, who is working here
in Little Horn."

"Casper? He sure wants that valley—I mean real
bad. And once he has it, he can sell it to the railroad."

Clint Adams was already shaking his head. "He wants
the land. And that's it. I don't think he even wants
gold—if there were any, which I doubt. He just wants
to go on being what he is: a cattleman. Chance Casper."

"Maybe."

"Not 'maybe.' He's being squeezed by the Eastern-
Western. I'll bet money on that. Fitzsimmons runs the
bank, or maybe he even owns it. The point is, he's the
big gun in town."

"I knew the Eastern-Western was here. I didn't know
Tennessee Fitz was about."

"He is—about."

"So maybe he is arranging the whiskey to the tribes,
and the gold-or-not-gold strike that is about to hit us,
to throw confusion, even chaos, all over the place, thus
giving the Eastern-Western the chance to push for a
marshal they can handle. Not a man such as yourself,
I'd say."

"They'll pull in millions bringing in those immigrants," Clint said.

"How come Knox Hollinger got in their way," Mulholland pointed out.

"And now?"

"And now you are in their way."

"Darling Feetz! I am reech!"

Those words broke jubilantly from the Countess Maritza as she sat stark naked on the edge of Tennessee
Fitz's bed and let her eyes play on his bare buttocks as
he stepped into his long-handled underwear.

Her attention, however, was no longer on sex, for
she had been well satisfied, and so her thoughts had
swiftly returned to the "excuse" for their celebration:
the news that the law would uphold her claim to her
dead husband's land; followed by the news that more
than just likely there was gold to be dug on just that
acreage.

"My cup ees full!" She was almost crying with joy.
"It is your help that did it, Feetz."

He stood looking down at her. "Not just my help, my
dear. It took a lot more than just help. And you will not
forget the paper that you signed for me last night."

"The paper?"

"Yes, while we were enjoying our champagne."

"I don't remember . . . or, oh yes, I sign something.
What? What was it I sign, Feetz?"

"We'll go into that later, my dear. Meanwhile, you
must enjoy your happiness. But remember, it is not
certain—not absolutely certain—about the gold
situation. Which is why you signed the power of
attorney. Do not forget that, my dear."

But she was dancing about the room, hardly hearing
him as the thought of owning the land clearly, the land
that Serge had claimed, swept through her.

"Now then," he said, slipping into his coat, "I have much to do. I have to see the lawyer again, and I have many people to see, my dear."

She came toward him, still only half-dressed. "Till I see you again, my dear one." She melted against him as his arms encircled her.

His passion began to rise, but he controlled himself. It was a big day lying ahead. It was a day when the whole business, the entire plan, could turn. And it would turn, by heaven. It would turn, if people would just do as they had been instructed.

"You can stay here, my dear, and Stamper will bring you breakfast. But don't go out without letting myself or Stamper know. I have a number of visitors coming to see me on business, and, uh . . ." He let it hang while she grinned mischievously at him.

"You will make all the mens jelly!" She grinned wickedly.

"*Jealous*," he corrected. "Just think of tonight. Tonight we're really going to celebrate!"

He stepped out of the bedroom into the corridor and walked down to his office.

On the way, he ran into Stamper.

"Did he get here?"

"He has been waiting, sir."

"How long?"

"I'd say more than half an hour."

"Good. Just listen for my bell."

Tennessee Fitz strode down to the end of the corridor and entered the room to find the Reverend Crispus Quinn, garbed suitably in his black religious garments, smoking a cigar. Fitz realized instantly that it was one of his own, undoubtedly taken from the humidor box on his desk.

He frowned.

"A good cigar, Fitz, is the next best thing to a good woman," Crisp Quinn said, leaving his unctuous role for a moment and returning to more jolly times.

"I haven't had breakfast yet, Quinn. You might join me for coffee if you've a mind to. There's a lot to talk about."

"Praise the Lord for good cigars, good coffee and whiskey, and bad women," intoned the Reverend Quinn, rolling his large eyes toward heaven.

Tennessee Fitz chuckled right along with him. It was going to be a big day. A good day. It was going to be his!

The breakfast finished, Stamper had removed the tray and brought fresh coffee. The two men reached the meat of their conversation. They discussed details, plans; the work with the connection in Cheyenne and the man in Washington; the situation with the whiskey wagon and the Indians, and the brouhaha that was already being raised over the wanton murder of a Shoshone who had been drinking and gambling—and had lost all round. Surely the government, representing the will of the people, would no longer tolerate these ignorant barbarians in their midst and would move their reservation far away from Little Horn.

They discussed the possibility of gold near Chance Casper's spread.

"None whatever," Tennessee put it.

"You sure of that?" Crisp Quinn was feeling delightful

after that fine cigar and that good coffee. He'd had two cups.

"I know it. It is—or at any rate, it will be—what is known as a diversionary tactic," Fitz explained. "There will be a mad stampede for gold, and when it is revealed that there isn't a grain of it within a hundred miles, there will be the reaction: relief, in a way. Disillusionment, however, will then take over, and they—those who got so exercised over becoming rich—they will turn toward a leader. You."

Crisp Quinn beamed. "I shall lead them out of the dark valley of despair. Amen!"

"They will be eating from our hands. And they will then be eager to turn toward work, building and setting up houses on the lots that we have already mapped out. Meanwhile, I have received notice from the authorities that the savages will be removed."

"Where to?"

Fitz waved a hand. "West, somewhere."

"And Casper and his 88 Slash?"

"The bank will close." A big grin spread across Tennessee Fitz's face.

They were silent for a moment, each contemplating the campaign that was drawing swiftly to its conclusion.

Presently, Tennessee Fitz spoke. He spoke very quietly, his eyes watching his visitor carefully.

"There is something on your mind, Crispus."

"The Gunsmith. Adams."

"I thought so. Well, that is all arranged. Adams will not bother us."

"But you remember, Fitz, that you promised something."

"I haven't forgotten. It was a definite part of our agreement, Crispus. And I am a man of my word. I think you will agree with me there, won't you?"

"I surely hope so."

"It's all arranged. And there is no reason why it should not go exactly as planned."

Tennessee Fitz leaned back, reaching into his waistcoat. He took out his gold watch and looked at it.

"Midmorning," he said. "And we've been cooped up in here all this time. I have no notion where the idea started, my friend. But I have heard so often that these events are supposed to take place at high noon. Do you see it that way?"

"I do. Of course, the other party has to realize it as well."

"Well, if you agree to that hour. Then we can see that the other party receives the message."

He slipped his big gold watch back into his waistcoat pocket and, turning his back on Crispus Quinn, walked to the window of his office and stood there, looking out at the enormous sky.

Silence invaded the room. Neither of them was even smoking. Crispus Quinn, always a man of swift perception, realized that the meeting was over.

"Until later," he said to the back that was facing him.

There was no answer. There was no more to be said. The meeting was over.

And yet, Crispus Quinn lingered. He was struggling. For as he stood there looking at that broad back by the window, he began to feel himself quite differently than he ever had before in all his years.

He wanted, suddenly more than anything he had ever

wanted in his whole life, to say something. Just to ask, maybe, the simple question. That it would be all right. That it had all been thoroughly planned, and that there was no chance of a mistake. He bit his lip, for there was indeed that other part that refused.

But suddenly the man at the window spoke, without turning around; he spoke with his back still facing into the room.

"It will be all right, Crispus. Everything has been taken care of."

"Of course," the Black Ace, the Fastest Gun of Them All replied, his voice barely above a whisper. His hand, he realized, was clammy as it touched the doorknob and turned it.

But it was clearly too late to go back. The Great Gunfighter who would go down in history had only one direction he could take.

It was Professor Obediah Turpin—otherwise or formerly known as Ace LeJeune—who brought the news to the Gunsmith, having his breakfast in the O.K. Cafe.

His presence was requested in the middle of Main Street at high noon.

"Where did you get this?" Clint Adams asked as he took a drink of coffee.

"One of the swampers from the Pastime brought it. Said to pass it on to you."

"Why didn't he bring it to me himself?"

"Said he didn't know where to locate you. And he seen us together that time we were in the . . . I can't recollect. Wherever it was."

"Sounds fishy."

"That's not my worry."

"I won't be there. You can tell him or not."

"He's real fast, that feller," Turpin said.

"So let him pick on somebody his own size. I'm getting old and rusty. And besides, I don't accept challenges. That's a stupid thing. Tell him to go to hell."

"That your last word?"

"Nope. You can tell Tennessee Fitz to . . . let's see . . ." He had suddenly remembered something that Felice had said. "Yeah. Tell him to go sit on a tack." He grinned at Obediah Turpin.

Professor Turpin gave a curt nod, sucked his teeth, and took his departure.

But Clint knew that was only the beginning.

It was clear that Fitz was forcing a showdown. Probably to work in with the gold situation and the Indian question, for there would be an outcry against the murder of the Shoshone—not so much that anybody cared among the whites, but because it might bring retaliations.

Well, he was thinking, he could leave town. But that still wouldn't find him Knox Hollinger's killer.

He had hardly heard Felice come in from the kitchen. "There's some men gathered outside the Pastime," she told him. "It doesn't look good."

"What do you mean?"

"They don't look like they're going to a wedding."

She was a little pale, he thought. "Where's Emile?"

"That lazy lout is s'posed to be here."

The door opened and Emile was there.

"There is a crowd out there. There are men with guns. What is to be done?"

"I'll finish my coffee," the Gunsmith said. "If anyone wants to speak to me, he can come here."

"Not here!" cried Emile. "They will wreck this place!"

"I guess you're right," Clint said. He lifted his cup, looking at Emile and Felice as they stood there with their eyes loaded, and he said, "Here's luck to you both!" He drank the toast of coffee.

Emile had gone to the window. "The crowd is not more."

"*No more*," Felice corrected. "The crowd is *no more*. Or the crowd is no longer there."

"It's vamoose."

Clint checked his six-gun and shook his hands loose. Then, opening the door of the cafe, he stepped out into the street. The street was empty as he started along the boardwalk.

There was still nobody in sight. His eyes scanned the roofs, and passing an alley he moved quickly. But he didn't hurry. He felt loose. He knew, somehow, where it would be. Up by the Pastime, where the crowd had been earlier.

Get off the wood, he thought. Get into the street, but not too far, not where he could be crossfired.

So Crisp Quinn had thrown down the challenge. That meant one thing. There would be more than one gun working . . . for Tennessee Fitz.

Well, he could have left town. But that would have solved nothing. It never occurred to him, except as part of the short list going through his head of what might be a possibility. He could run, he could try to hide, or he could face it. Of course, he could just ignore the whole thing, but the result would be the same. Somehow, some way, somebody would face him; and it would surely be somebody with backup. The question was who. He had a pretty good notion who would be siding Quinn. But the question was how. And the question was still who had killed Knox Hollinger?

He was just about even with the Pastime now, and he saw the glint from the rifle barrel on the roof. He stopped in his tracks, looking across at the man who had appeared in the saloon doorway.

"Gunsmith!"

It was the Black Ace, black from head to foot, except for his very white face and gray goatee. He was wearing a brace of Colts with chased silver grips in a Mexican crossrig.

"I am calling you, Gunsmith!"

A part of Clint's attention was on the rifle on the roof above Cratchett's Hardware. For a split second he was caught, but he pulled back just in time, remembering that no halfway sensible drygulcher would let his rifle barrel reflect sunlight like that. There had to be at least one other.

And suddenly the Reverend Crispus Quinn, the Fastest Gun in the West, struck for his gun.

Clint Adams—the Gunsmith now—caught the other movement in the window of the Pastime, and as that sly drygulcher pulled down on him, the Gunsmith shot him right in the head. Then he shot Crisp Quinn, who had dropped one gun but was firing the other all over the street, while those hardy souls who had chosen to be onlookers dove for cover. Crisp Quinn lay in the street, his face twisted in pain. Yet the pain in his arm was not as bad as the pain in the region of his heart. The

Gunsmith had simply shot him out of the action instead
of merely killing him. The humiliation might be harder
to bear than outright death. But the Gunsmith did not
like taking advantage of amateurs.

He said so now as he stood over the fallen gladiator,
lying in the dust with his black gun suit in total disarray.

Clint walked over to the man who had shot from the
window of the Pastime. As he had suspected, the body
was that of Professor Obediah Turpin.

A few people had started to come slowly into the
street. One of the first to reach Clint was Felice, who
all but fell into his arms, the tears of relief streaming
from her eyes.

Except that Clint Adams knew it wasn't over, after
all. The Gunsmith caught the flash of metal, from the
marshal's office this time. But the bullet intended for
him went into the blue sky. For swifter than silk, he
had drawn and shot Virgil Mulholland right through the
chest.

Two riders on buckskin ponies were coming slowly
down the street now, each wearing the badge of a United
States marshal.

"Looks like we got here for the big event," one of
them said. "What's going on?"

"I reckon they'll tell you I shot in self-defense," Clint
Adams said. "Anyway, if you're looking for the man
who murdered Knox Hollinger, that's him lying yonder."

"Can you prove that?" the other marshal asked.

"My gun proved it. He's still alive. Let him tell you
what he has to. But if you still have any question about it,
ask him where he got that buckskin vest that I gave Knox
Hollinger when we were working together in Laramie."

• • •

"And you knew all along that the Mulholland man was working with Fitzsimmons? And that it was he who murdered Knox?"

They were sitting in the kitchen at Knox Hollinger's place, now Norah's. She had just handed him a fresh mug of coffee.

"I knew something was out of whack when I spotted that buckskin vest. Knox wouldn't have given a man like that the weather. Then I remembered that Mulholland used to hire his gun to the stockgrowers, the Association."

"And what about the other man?" she asked.

"The professor?"

"The other one that tried to shoot you."

"Well, I knew Quinn was going to need plenty of backup. He's a kid; but a damn dangerous kid. But I figured whoever was behind him would see to it that he was not only covered once but twice."

"Twice?" she asked, her lovely brown eyes searching across his face. "Why two times?"

"Because anyone can figure you'll maybe have backup. But Tennessee Fitz, I saw, was a man who overlooked nothing. Nothing! And so, being that careful, he just had to see to it that the backup man had backup."

"Clever," she said, smiling at him, but it was a smile of grand relief. "I was frightened by the whole thing. I saw it. Tom and I were there."

"Why? How come you were there?"

"I don't know." She looked down at her hands. "Just . . . well, somehow, something in me wanted to come in to town to see you. I felt upset; sort of like something was going to happen, but I couldn't put it into words. And—and Tom noticed I was like that and insisted on coming along."

"Are you sorry?"

"I'm glad."

"Do you feel that something's going to happen now?"

"Yes. Oh yes, I do."

"Something . . ."

"With someone . . ." Her smile was radiant. Her brown eyes were shining as he came to her and she stood up.

Later, as they lay together resting, she said, "And Tennessee Fitzsimmons? What will happen to him?"

"The marshals arrested him. Now the law will handle it. Sooner or later they catch up. It's a law."

She reached over and put her hand on his chest. "I know another law," she said.

"Tell me. I'm ready, willing, and I hope able to learn."

"I think," she whispered, with her lips against his ear, "I think it would be best for me to demonstrate."

Watch for

KILLER'S RACE

109th novel in the exciting GUNSMITH series
from Jove

Coming in January!

A special offer for people who enjoy reading the best
Westerns published today. If you enjoyed this book,
subscribe now and get . . .

TWO FREE

A $5.90 VALUE—NO OBLIGATION

If you enjoyed this book and would like to read more
of the very best Westerns being published today, you'll want
to subscribe to True Value's Western Home Subscription
Service. If you enjoyed the book you just read and want more
of the most exciting, adventurous, action packed Westerns,
subscribe now.

Each month the editors of True Value will select the 6
very best Westerns from America's leading publishers for
special readers like you. You'll be able to preview these new
titles as soon as they are published, FREE for ten days with
no obligation.

TWO FREE BOOKS

When you subscribe, we'll send you your first month's
shipment of the newest and best 6 Westerns for you to
preview. With your first shipment, two of these books will
be yours as our introductory gift to you absolutely FREE,
regardless of what you decide to do. If you like them, as much
as we think you will, keep all six books but pay for just 4 at the
low subscriber rate of just $2.45 each. If you decide to return
them, keep 2 of the titles as our gift. No obligation.

Special Subscriber Savings

When you become a True Value subscriber you'll save
money several ways. First, all regular monthly selections will
be billed at the low subscriber price of just $2.45 each. That's

WESTERNS!

at least a savings of $3.00 each month below the publishers price. Second, there is never any shipping, handling or other hidden charges—Free home delivery. What's more there is no minimum number of books you must buy, you may return any selection for full credit and you can cancel your subscription at any time. A TRUE VALUE!

Mail the coupon below

To start your subscription and receive 2 FREE WESTERNS, fill out the coupon below and mail it today. We'll send your first shipment which includes 2 FREE BOOKS as soon as we receive it.

J.R. ROBERTS
THE
GUNSMITH